I0714394

TEARS FOR JESSIE HEWITT

Edna Sherry

Black Gat Books

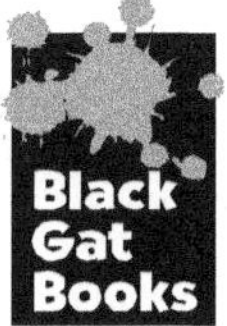

Black Gat Books • Eureka California

NO TEARS FOR JESSIE HEWITT

Published by Black Gat Books
A division of Stark House Press
1315 H Street
Eureka, CA 95501, USA
griffinskye3@sbcglobal.net
www.starkhousepress.com

NO TEARS FOR JESSIE HEWITT
Originally published in by Dodd, Mead and Company, New York, and copyright © 1958 by Edna Sherry. Reprinted in paperback as *She Asked for Murder* by Dell Books, New York, 1959.

ISBN-13: 978-1-951473-36-5

Book design by Jeff Vorzimmer, *¡caliente!design*, Austin, Texas
Proofreading by Bill Kelly
Cover art by Robert Stanley

First Stark House Press/Black Gat Edition: June 2021

Dedication:
To Ernie With Love

PROLOGUE

Meg Wiley eyed her two men to see that they were presentable for appearance at a church wedding: Lance—lieutenant at Homicide East when he was working—and Sandy, age eight, all eyelashes, cowlick and freckles. She nodded a cool approval. She would have died before admitting that she considered each in his way the most perfect specimen on earth. Her two men were more vocal. Sandy said, "Nobody'll notice us with you around, Mommy."

And Lance smiled, "The kid's right, Beauty."

She was not beautiful but she felt she was, since they thought so.

As it was a Saturday and Lance's day off, the occasion was a special one. The wedding took second place as a festivity, the first being that the three of them would be together for a gratifying number of hours. They expressed this satisfaction in their different ways.

"Woo-hoo," Sandy hooted. "We're an island all by ourselves."

"Families are something," Lance grinned.

Meg, the introspective one, asked, "Lance, is it anti-social to be so terribly satisfied alone together?"

The wedding was in Westchester County at four o'clock. Since it was now only one p.m. and an unusually mild winter's day, they had a dividend of three delectable hours before them. They made no plans. Lance brought the Chevy around, tucked them into the front seat and drove aimlessly to the Parkway from the Riverdale section where they lived.

"Any suggestions?" he asked.

"Just give the car its head," said Meg comfortably.

"I don't like the Parkway much," Sandy put in.

Lance poked him with an elbow. "I know what's eating you, young Sandy. No signs on the Parkway, so you can't show off how well you can read."

It was true enough. Sandy was a word addict. At three, he had no use for any toys but lettered blocks; at four, he knew the alphabet; at five, he could read words; and at six, books. Now, at eight, he was refining his knack into a real skill. He could spell any word in ordinary use correctly and his memory was prodigious.

Meg, fearful of raising a pedantic little prig, would groan in private to Lance, "I will *not* have a darned Quiz Kid in the family. One of those uncanny little devils who roll up fortunes on TV. Can you imagine what they're like to live with?"

"Don't worry about Sandy," he would tell her easily. "He can throw a curve that even I have to reach for. And hold his own in any scrap in the schoolyard. He's all boy, even if he could cop $64,000 without blinking."

Sandy took his father's gibe about the Parkway good-humoredly but seriously, "Signs are pie. They're no test. What I don't like about the Parkway is there's only trees. I like to drive places where you can see people's houses."

"You're right, Sandy," Meg said. "The Parkway's fine for the driver but a little monotonous for the passengers."

So Lance turned off at an exit, found his way to a secondary road, then turned off that into a still narrower one, always bearing north in the general direction of their ultimate destination. They went through a busy little center called Herring and Lance wondered aloud if the natives were all pickled. Sandy, a satisfactory audience, giggled appreciatively. Later, they came to a sign that read:

CRAWFEY
SETTLED 1731
DRIVE CAREFULLY

Sandy savored the name on his tongue, "Crawfey. Crawfey. What a nutty name."

Instantly Lance whipped out a handkerchief, threw it across his arm in the pose of a waiter and chanted, "Tea, cocoa, milk or Crawfey?"

Sandy collapsed in laughter. A few minutes later, Meg, looking out at the passing village, cried in amazement, "Lance, look! The houses are pure Elizabethan. What a delightful spot."

"What's pure Elizabethan, Mommy?" asked Sandy, a sponge for information.

"Elizabeth was Queen of England about four hundred years ago, and in her reign they built houses like these—dark wood with white upper stories striped with black beams, so they still call them Elizabethan after her."

"Was she nice?"

"Oh, yes. In fact, they still call her Good Queen Bess."

They were out of the village now, and Sandy, relegating Crawfey and the Virgin Queen to the back of his mind, turned hopefully to Lance, "This is a good chance to play the Game, Daddy." Sandy's ambition in life was to be a detective under Lieutenant Wiley of Homicide, and the Game was a test in police probing.

"Okay," Lance agreed. "Let's see, now. How's this? An old lady, living alone, is found gagged and tied in her apartment one evening, and a considerable amount of money stolen. Okay. Use your brain."

Sandy began the first of the twenty questions he was allowed: "She live alone?"

"One bad mark, Sergeant. I already told you she did, but she has two nephews who live together a few blocks away. They visit her regularly. In fact, Larry found her and gave the alarm."

"How'd he get in?"

"Both Larry and Dick had keys, but Larry didn't

need one; the thief left the front door ajar."

"How'd the thief get in—I mean, any marks?"

"None."

"Where were the nephews at the time of the robbery?"

"Dick was sick in bed with a cold, and Larry at a movie."

"Any proof ?"

"No, just their own statements, except that when Larry phoned to tell Dick about it, Dick was still in bed."

"Uh—let's see—when did they see her before the robbery?"

"They took turns visiting her. The robbery was on a Wednesday night. Monday was Larry's night. The night before, Tuesday, Dick had been there. The old lady says he had the cold then, and she made him promise to do something for it and stay in bed."

"Is there a doorman?"

"Yes. He swears nobody suspicious came in by the front door or went up in the elevator, and the service entrance was locked."

"What does the old lady say?"

"She was watching TV and all of a sudden a bag was dropped over her head so she couldn't see. Then she was gagged and bound, but not injured. Larry arrived an hour later."

"What time was that?"

"Eight p.m."

"He got *out* of a movie at eight o'clock?"

"It was a newsreel, and he left early because he was due at his aunt's."

"Did the burglar talk—warn her, I mean?"

"No. Just went about his business."

"How many questions have I had?"

"Eleven. Nine to go."

"If she couldn't see or hear—did she feel anything—like f'rinstance, the kind of clothes he wore?"

"Nope."

"Well, did she smell anything?"

"She did, at that. She says she smelled whisky."

"The nephews drink?"

"No."

"The doorman?"

"No. Signed the pledge as a kid."

"Was he there every second—I mean—uh—didn't he have to go to the bathroom or something?"

"He may have, I guess."

"Okay. Arrest Dick."

"Good boy! You win. Now state the Clue."

"The liquor smell. That's what he did for his cold. As soon as Larry went to the movies, Dick hustled over to his aunt's and watched till the doorman took a break—went up—and used a bag over her head so she shouldn't see him. Then he snuck back home and was in bed again when Larry phoned about the robbery."

"Nice work, Sergeant Wiley," said Lance, saluting. Sandy wriggled with delight and did his best to sound modest as he uttered the slogan that capped the Game:

"It just takes brains."

CHAPTER ONE

"It just takes brains," Francis Edwards smiled to himself. He sat in the plane, looking down at Philadelphia as it diminished below him. He had cause for his complacency. The job had been a success. He had brought it off as planned, he was $7,200 richer, he was clear of the town before any hue and cry had been raised, and he had left no clues behind him.

There had been only one flaw in the whole

undertaking. At the last minute, that unruly violent second-self of his had flared up and nearly spoiled a perfect piece of work. Up until then, it had been such a smooth operation; thought out to the last detail.

First, he had checked in at the plush hotel and lived there for ten days, establishing himself as a solid, solvent guest, before making a move. Then he had sent himself a telegram purporting to be from his boss, ordering him to Rio at once. He had made it his business to drop this information to the desk clerk as he settled his bill and discussed plane facilities to South America. (He already had his reservation, under another name, for the, 4:45 flight to Chicago.)

The next step was a phone call to a leading used-car dealer, offering him a super-Jaguar at a sacrifice for immediate cash.

"I'm rushed for time," he explained. "Can't even drive the car down to your place or go to the bank with a check, so if you want a bargain, be here in half an hour with the cash. The name's Edwards, room 602." (If the dealer was a careful operator, he would call the hotel and check. And the desk clerk would give him a clean bill.)

The dealer did just that and arrived within twenty minutes. But he was not alone. There was a big young redhead with him.

"My assistant," the dealer said. "Brought him along to drive your car back if we make the deal."

Edwards smiled and nodded as he ushered them into his room and closed the door. Then his gun was out and he ordered them both against the wall. The dealer was sensible and submitted without protest. But, as Edwards was taping his mouth, the redhead burst out with a flood of scalding abuse, full of contempt.

It was then that the unruly second-self of Edwards saw red at the slap at his ego and battered down with the gun butt, not once but again and again, until the redhead toppled like a tree falling.

Satisfied with his ferocious interlude, the second-self sank back into limbo and allowed Edwards to finish the job with cool efficiency. He bound the gagged men hand and foot, rifled their wallets, dusted the whole room to remove all prints, picked up his packed suitcase, and left the hotel. He walked three blocks before he hailed a roving taxi and drove to the Thirtieth Street Station. He walked through the waiting room, out another entrance, put several blocks between himself and the station, then took another cab to the airport. He made the Chicago plane in comfortable time, leaving such a confused trail behind him that he would be hard, if not impossible, to trace.

But his satisfaction with a job well done was marred by the memory of the gun butt cracking against the redhead's skull. He was no killer, violence was no part of his policy. He carried a gun to scare his victims, without any real intention of using it. Even that second-self of his hadn't gone so far as to pull the trigger—had only hit out in his outraged vanity.

He settled himself more comfortably in his seat. His natural optimism came to the fore. The redhead had a thick shock of hair. Probably he had only stunned him. And if he suffered a slight concussion, it would teach him not to belittle a clever man soon again.

In Chicago he left the plane and checked into a decent obscure hotel for the night. Next morning, using the name Victor Clyde, he bought a stunning mauve year-old Cadillac, in which he would start a leisurely trip to the Coast. It was December 16th, and Santa Anita did not open until the 28th, when he would begin his real campaign. The car-dealer episode had been only an isolated stunt to provide him with a stake. The racetrack was his real field of action, although he rarely bet on a horse. It was the other fellow's bets which would line his pockets.

As soon as he was clear of the town, he pulled over to the side of the road to scan the Chicago papers he had brought along. News of the Philadelphia escapade would hardly travel this far west unless it had ended in the murder of the redhead. There was nothing. Whistling, he drove on in the smooth-purring Cadillac.

He was thirty-two years old, with pleasing features, thick dark hair and blue eyes, but a man who would have gone unnoticed except for his sharply marked dark eyebrows and his excess of vitality, a kind of animal magnetism which pointed up his every look and word. His tritest assertions (and he was no mental giant) took on color and authenticity from this inner voltage; men listened to him and women yielded to him—and both enjoyed the process.

Originally he had come of decent Ohio farm stock, submitting with outward good-humor to his father's insistence on a degree of education, but secretly determined to break away from the stodgy rural life as soon as opportunity offered. At eighteen he welcomed the draft, which took him first to boot camp, and then to active service in the Pacific. A few bloody but successful skirmishes with Japs taught him the absolute power of a gun. The thing was psychological. There was rarely any need to shoot. The mere sight of a gun could subdue half a dozen surprised men.

After the war, having no special skills or professional training, he decided that this playing on men's fears was a livelier way of getting money than working. The danger and excitement gave color to his life, and a successful foray enlarged his already sizable portrait of himself. The occasional need to flee the district of his crime fed his restless spirit with the stimulus of new scenes. He enjoyed transient fellowship in bars, hotels, or at ball-games, but never made a permanent friend.

He was very free with money. He loved to pick up the tab for drinks or dinner with any chance group he found himself in. He was a soft touch for any sum from five dollars to five hundred. He found ample reward in the admiration and attention his beneficiaries accorded him. All over the country, men and women whom he had known only for an hour or a day remembered him warmly and hoped they would run into him again. But he shed them deliberately: they had served their purpose by listening to him with flattering respect. This hunger in him was sharper than any other appetite.

He never gave an address or received mail. The only letter he had written in ten years was a note long ago to his father, stating that he preferred the Far East to America and would not return.

He was a complete extrovert. He liked good food, spectator sports, beer, TV, handsome cars, and smart clothes. Women played an unimportant part in his life, as is generally the case with egotists. He could take them or leave them alone. Besides, he sensed the danger of their curiosity and intuition. He was a lone wolf in his criminal forays and confided in nobody. Up to now, he had never been caught, but he had had one or two frightening shaves.

He made a tourist's holiday of his trip west, stopping at beauty spots on the road, either in high-class motels or first-rate hotels, enjoying every minute of picking up temporary companions and forgetting them next day. When, at last, he reached Los Angeles, he rented a small comfortable garden apartment, its ground-floor entrance ensuring privacy for his comings and goings.

On opening day at Santa Anita, he drove to the track, one of many thousands eager for the beginning of the racing season. He avoided the clubhouse. Too many track detectives were on guard there, protecting the film stars who studded the enclosure. But there was plenty of money in the grandstand, too, even if its spenders were less distinguished.

He sauntered along the broad aisle between the grandstand and the mutuel windows. At the end of the line, across from the fifty-dollar window, he located some benches where the overflow crowd from the grandstand salvaged sitting room. He settled himself, opened his *Racing Form*, and prepared to watch the fifty-dollar window over its edge. He was too far away to hear anything, or even to see exactly what money passed into the grille, but the ticket-seller's shoulder and arm were visible enough for him to count the number of times he pressed the lever as he served any given buyer. Most people bought only one fifty-dollar ticket, or at most, two. They were not Victor Clyde's meat. Patiently he waited until a real prospect came along.

Naturally he would have preferred to deal with bettors at the hundred-dollar window, but there was too much against it. First, at most tracks the hundred-dollar windows were housed in a small cabin-like enclosure where it was impossible for him to follow any details of the transactions. Second, at the door to these cubicles there was usually a policeman or Pinkerton man on duty. And third, over the years he had observed an odd quirk in racetrack human nature: a man who bet a hundred dollars on a race usually preferred buying two fifty-dollar tickets to one hundred-dollar ticket. Victor figured that the presence of the uniformed officer scared them off—if they won a sizable bet, mightn't the cop tip off the income-tax people? Or was it that, if they collected at the hundred-dollar window, they feared pickpockets? Whatever the reason, he had not done badly sticking to the fifty-dollar patrons.

The horses were on the track and nearing the gate when a likely victim appeared at the window. The seller's shoulder dipped time and again as he ground out ticket after ticket. Clyde counted ten times. Five hundred dollars on a two-year-old maiden race. This was for him.

Leisurely he rose, spotted the man as he shoved the thick sheaf of tickets into the pocket of his gay flowered sport shirt. A careless man, Clyde noted with satisfaction. He looked to be about thirty-five, undistinguished, but with a nebulous aura which related him to the film world. Probably a well-paid engineer or art worker, Victor decided, but not part of the social merry-go-round, else he would be in the Clubhouse, hobnobbing with the noblesse.

Unobtrusively, he followed the man to his seat in the stand, took up a coign of vantage in the aisle and watched him. At the end of the race, the man tossed away the bundle of tickets as carelessly as he had pocketed them. Before the next race started, he went again to the fifty-dollar window and again bought a thick packet of tickets. Twice, Victor saw him go to the cashier's window, once when the winning horse paid a $19.80 mutuel, netting him more than four thousand dollars. Victor watched this with regret. Four thousand dollars would have made a neat haul but the time for action was not yet.

After the sixth race, the man began to look at his wrist watch at frequent intervals. Victor took this as a sign that he was due back in Hollywood and would not stay for the last race. With relief, he found he was right. The man bought his seventh-race tickets and then went toward the stairs. He stuffed the tickets as negligently as before in his shirt pocket, to be cashed or tossed away the next day.

Victor went for his own car, keeping a weather eye out for his quarry. He watched him enter a baby-blue Chrysler convertible, as gay as his flowered shirt.

He was easy to follow, much more so than he would have been in the massive traffic after the last race. Rather to his surprise, the man headed, not toward Hollywood, but toward a good residential section of Glendale. He turned into the driveway of a pleasing, but not sumptuous, house, set in ample grounds; parked, and entered, using a key. Victor hoped this was a sign that the man lived alone, but he knew it was no real proof.

Victor drove on, parked a block away and sat patiently in his car with the house in view. A long hour's wait finally rewarded him. The man, now in dinner clothes, came out, got into his car and drove away. As soon as he was out of sight, Victor walked past the house, scrutinizing the mail box which read, "Lex Carver." He went back to his car and drove away, stopping at a drugstore to look up Lex Carver in the phone book and call the house. There was no answer.

Satisfied, he drove home, showered, dressed, and went out for a good dinner. It looked as if he had a live prospect and a few days' patience would be rewarding. What was more, he enjoyed every moment of it, satisfying some infantile itch for cops-and-robbers excitement.

For the rest of the week Victor went to the races. On all but one day Carver was there, too. Now, however, he gave Carver a wide berth and spent his time, not near the selling windows, but near enough to the fifty-dollar cashiers' grille to see when Carver won a bet. On Saturday, the crucial moment arrived. The third-race payoff was $43.20, and, to his delight, he saw Carver approach the cashier's window, a pleased grin on his face and the usual thick wad of tickets in his hand. Even across the aisle, he could hear the cashier stamp ticket after ticket as he paid Carver off. He figured that Carver must have won something like $10,000 on the race. And, unless he piddled it away on the next four or five races, the pickings should be good.

Victor left the track immediately, drove to Glendale, parked a few doors down from Carver's home, went on foot to the nearest drugstore, and called the house. As before, there was no answer. He took a small zippered bag containing his "props" from the trunk of his car, walked to the house, up the driveway, and around to the back where a growth of eucalyptus trees all but blocked out the kitchen door. With a strip of celluloid, he pushed back the simple lock without trouble and was inside. Stealthily, he made a tour of the split-level house and satisfied himself that he was in sole possession.

He knew he had a long wait before him, but just in case someone turned up in the interval, he began his preparations so that he would be ready for all eventualities. From the zippered bag he took a pair of paint-smeared coveralls and slipped into them. They hid his well-cut sports clothes and turned him into an anonymous workman. Then he took a package of Band-Aids from the bag and applied one to each finger. He had found that they impeded him less than gloves and successfully prevented leaving fingerprints. He slipped his gun into one coverall pocket, a roll of adhesive tape, twine, and a small scissors in the other, and was ready for his man; except for adjusting the Hallowe'en mask over his face and hair, which he would do at the sound of Carver's car outside.

He went into the bedroom and settled himself comfortably in an easy chair. It was characteristic of him that he was placid and relaxed during the wait. Speed and tension would come later during the actual encounter, but until then he made no demands on his nervous system.

It was dark before the crunch of tires on gravel reached his ears. Darkness was an added asset, since he could leave the house and the neighborhood with less risk of being seen. He pulled on the grotesque plastic mask, stepped behind the open bedroom door and waited.

The front door opened and closed. Footsteps approached and crossed the bedroom as Carver made his way to the bathroom to wash up. Victor let him reach the wash basin with his back turned before he stepped after him, gun pointed, and said quietly: "Reach, brother. This is a stick-up."

Carver whirled, stared, and then grinned.

"Bill, you son of a gun, at your old tricks, huh?" He broke off as the gun bored into his stomach.

Victor said grimly: "The safety catch is off. It's your life."

Carver's jaw dropped and his hands went slowly up. "An honest-to-God holdup!" he muttered.

"Right. Now step into the bathtub and lie on your face with your hands behind you."

Carver obeyed, less from fright than from the dictates of common sense. Swiftly Victor plastered his mouth, strapped his wrists together, and tied his ankles with the stout twine. When Carver was completely helpless, Victor turned him over on his back, reached for his bulging wallet, and transferred the money to his own pocket. He searched Carver's coat and trousers pockets, bringing out the overflow which the wallet could not accommodate. Evidently his luck had held up since the third race. Having done the job with ruthless efficiency, Victor's besetting weakness came to the fore. Even as a burglar he wanted to be liked.

"Got an address book around?" he asked.

Carver nodded, jerking his head toward the bedroom.

"Okay. In an hour I'll call somebody to come and release you." He brought the book from the bedroom, read a name aloud: "Stan Agnew?" Carver shook his head. "Bill Bannerman?" Carver nodded vigorously. "Okay. It's been a pleasure."

He went to the kitchen, pulled off the mask, took a dirty painter's cap from the zipper bag and put it on. He let himself out of the kitchen door, leaving it ajar, slipped down the driveway, and back to his car. It was the dinner hour and he saw no one on the quiet residential street. In the car, he removed the cap and coveralls, put everything back in the zipper bag, pulled the Band-Aids off his fingers, and pocketed them. Then he drove home leisurely.

At his apartment, he let down the venetian blinds and adjusted the slats to defeat any prying eyes from the patio. He emptied his pockets in a lovely green shower on his bed and began the delightful job of counting it. There was fourteen thousand and eighty-two dollars. The biggest haul he had ever made. Santa Anita was "the most." Money in chunks. And you didn't have to waste sympathy on your victim. He was no worse off than he would have been if he had had a bad day at the track and gone home cleaned out by the mutuels, instead of by Victor Clyde.

He adjusted the cash in his money belt, washed up, and went back to his car. The first thing he did was to call Bill Bannerman, telling him to go and release his friend. Then he stopped into an attractive bar for a drink before dinner.

A quick glance told him that the most pleasing prospect in view was a girl in swirling flame-colored chiffon. He edged onto the stool beside her and ordered a Martini. His instinct was right. A minute later the girl took out a cigarette and made a futile attempt to light it with a lighter which was guaranteed not to work. Victor took out his own lighter, flicked it on and studied the girl while he lit her cigarette. She was very young, rather pretty, and, he thought, a tasty dish to cap a successful day. After two drinks she said her name was Ruby and that she had the evening free. He invited her to dinner.

He took her to a good place where he got immediate service by tipping the maître d' lavishly. This maneuver, the showy Cadillac, and the sumptuous dinner nearly tongue-tied the girl. Victor enjoyed her diffidence, but a heavier worry seemed to weigh upon her. This puzzled him. A free feed was all to the good but why did she linger over coffee so desperately, delaying the real business of the evening? Feeling that he could afford bluntness, he asked her outright. Her embarrassment caused her to bat her mascara'd eyelashes, and even to color under her make-up. She stammered, "Could we go to your place?"

"Why should we?" he asked coldly. He wanted nobody, even a casual pick-up, to connect him with a definite address.

Her explanation came out in an artless rush. Her earnings were sending a kid brother to a decent boarding school. But the Christmas holidays were not yet over and he was stopping with her.

"If he should happen to wake up—" she finished in a whisper. Then, with a wail of regret, "Just my luck to meet you this week!"

Victor ran true to form. He peeled a hundred-dollar bill off his roll and slipped it into her hand.

"Look. Stick with the kid till he goes back to school. No pick-ups. You hear? That's an order. Come on, I'll drive you home."

He hardly missed the physical pleasure he had forgone. The adoration in Ruby's eyes had fed a deeper hunger.

All in all, a perfect day.

CHAPTER TWO

Next day Victor scanned the papers with special interest. This, of course, was good sense. He had to learn how close behind him the police were. But there was an added reason: the account of his exploit gave him a tremendous lift; he cherished his clippings like a movie-star.

The robbery was reported more or less accurately. Considering the disguising properties of the Hallowe'en mask, Carver gave a remarkably precise description of Victor's age, height, build, and manner of speech. (But Victor knew that the mask successfully disguised the timbre of his voice.) What Carver did not report was the full amount of cash stolen, or that it was money he had won at the track. Victor guessed correctly that Carver had no wish to advertise to his employers how he spent a good many of his afternoons. The omission pleased Victor immensely. If the police connected the robbery with preliminary spadework at Santa Anita, they might keep an eye open for innocent-seeming observers at the track, might, indeed, spoil Victor's little racket for the rest of the meeting.

But the sharp-eyed Carver was responsible for giving Victor a nickname amusing enough to get into the headlines. Carver had noticed his hands, and in every paper, Victor was advertised as the "Band-Aid Bandit." This was not so good. Victor pondered on whether to resort to gloves in the future, or to work barehanded and depend on wiping off all surfaces he might touch in the course of a job. In the end he hit on a plan which tickled his rather crude sense of humor. He bought a box of foundation cream in a rachel color, and tinted the outside of the Band-Aids so that they blended with the color of his fingers and were hardly noticeable.

Nevertheless, during the next two months he

pulled only three more jobs. He was a moderate man, not given to excesses, and conceded the inevitability of the law of averages. He was a subscriber to the axioms about the pitcher and the well, and running a good thing into the ground. He was a reasonably competent craftsman except for the one weak link in his make-up—his vanity. A withering taunt against his brains and superiority brought out the latent devil in him which he deplored but could not always control. But that rarely happened: most men respected his gun enough to keep a civil tongue in their heads.

He spent his days at the track but it was a good while before he found another victim worthy of his steel, and who, at the same time, lived alone. His second job netted him only three thousand dollars and his third, nothing—the prospect having prudently dropped his winnings in the night slot of his bank on his way home from the races.

Early in March Victor took stock. He had close to eighteen thousand dollars, including the remains of the Philadelphia haul, and the meeting had only two weeks more to run. He decided to settle down in some charming place like La Jolla for a while and enjoy a holiday of swimming, sailing, and fishing, until the New York tracks were in full swing. But if he went to La Jolla he would want a smart little speed boat. One more haul would pay for it.

He spotted his quarry that very day at the track: an elderly, hard-bitten professional gambler who made one, or, at most, two bets a day, but those of fair size. And, Victor noted, he usually won. After two days of watching, Victor followed him home and discovered that he lived in a rather raffish sporting hotel called the Mengo, where comings and goings were not questioned, or even observed. Victor was able to ride up in the same elevator with him and note the number of his room without a curious glance from anyone. The one drawback was that the gambler usually bet favorites, and even a thousand-dollar bet would not net too much.

But on the third day, the fourth-race winner paid an even twelve dollars, and his man collected. Victor left the track immediately, made for the sporting hotel, and entered the man's room without a hitch. He had plenty of time for his usual routine of coveralls, Band-Aids, gun, and tape. The room was a single, so he felt comfortably sure his victim lived alone. At six o'clock he took up a position behind the bathroom door, adjusted his mask, and waited. But it was closer to seven when his man arrived and it was instantly apparent that there had been a few stops on the road to celebrate the winning of five thousand dollars. Victor nodded with satisfaction. A slightly tipsy man was easy to handle.

He waited as usual until the man entered the bathroom, then stepped out, and went through his routine. But the drinks had given the man enough Dutch courage to resist. Instead of obeying Victor's orders, he lunged at the mask and pulled hard. The elastic broke, the mask came off, and Victor stood revealed—marked and recognizable by the small, shrewd gray eyes of the gambler.

Nine crooks out of ten would have pulled the trigger, figuring it justifiable self-defense from their warped point of view. Victor did not. He struck out with his gun butt, hard enough to floor the man but with no intent to kill. He collected the man's cash and the mask, thrust his painter's cap low on his forehead, and let himself out of the room. He reached his car without incident and was home in twenty minutes.

The haul netted him a little over eight thousand dollars, but any elation he might have felt was wiped out by the danger he was in. He was no longer an anonymous figure in a clown's mask. He could be described and identified. The wise thing to do would be to pack his clothes, step into his car, and put as many miles as he could between himself and Los Angeles before his victim regained consciousness and alerted the police.

But the Philadelphia incident gave him pause. He had never discovered whether the car-dealer's redheaded assistant had lived or died, and the uncertainty still gnawed at him. He tried to remember how hard he had hit the gambler. He was easily past sixty and even a moderate blow might be fatal at that age. One thing was sure. He couldn't leave town before he knew what it was he faced—possible detection as a holdup man—or an all-out search for a murderer. He would wait only until he had seen the morning papers, and then be on his way. La Jolla was out. He would leave the State and put the whole continent between himself and the shrewd gray eyes of the gambler.

CHAPTER THREE

He read with relief, next morning, that the gambler, Herman Grotz, was alive. But it was with something a good deal less than relief that he learned how much the man had observed in the fractional time between his snatch at the mask and Victor's blow. Victor's thick brown hair, his regular features, his blue eyes and above all, his arched, well-marked eyebrows were described with frightening clarity.

He threw his packed suitcases into the trunk of the car and was on his way after a word to Olsen, the superintendent, that he was suddenly called to San Francisco by a death in the family and would not be back.

He was all the way across town when he realized that he had eaten no breakfast. He weighed the wisdom of eating in town against stopping at some roadside place along the way, and decided he would be less conspicuous in a busy city restaurant. It was a decision that changed his whole life.

He found himself in a maze of shabby streets, the stucco scaling from the small houses, the tiny grass-plots dusty. It was not a slum, it was just the dreary habitation of the thousands of Hollywood underlings who had not made the grade and who worked at the petty, anonymous jobs which form the foundation for the glittering façade of the fabulous city. It was past ten o'clock and the drudges were long since at their work. Along the streets blowsy wives—exhibiting fat thighs in their shorts—slouched along, carrying immense bags of groceries.

It was not an appetizing district, but Victor was hungry and stopped at the first decent eating-place he saw: a white-tiled, utilitarian, self-service establishment. To his surprise it was full, mostly with young men and girls who chattered like a group of jungle birds. As he pushed his tray along the assembly rail, he realized that he had stumbled into a rendezvous of unemployed movie extras, forgathered here in companionate misery. This was the substratum of the film world, the ragtag who lived on hope and dreams and an occasional check from home. He noted that before every one of them there was a cup of coffee and nothing more. He had his usual openhanded impulse to treat the whole roomful to a substantial meal. He desisted only because it would draw unwanted attention to himself.

With a full tray, he raked the room for a seat. In a far corner he spied a table for two with one empty place. He made his way to it and began transferring his dishes from the tray to the table without glancing at the occupied seat opposite. Only when he was seated did he glance across.

The girl sat, head bent, staring into her coffee cup. Her cheeks were wet with tears, and the thick dark lashes which hid her eyes stuck together in starlike points from the moisture. A crumpled letter lay on the table beside her. Normally a girl in a high-necked Dorothy Collins and wearing her slicked-back hair in a 1900 figure-eight wouldn't draw a second glance from Victor, but the tears caught his interest. He could never see any dilemma without being dead sure that he could solve it. He leaned forward and said pleasantly, "In trouble, sister?"

The friendly words seemed to panic her. Without looking up, she pushed the sugar bowl across to him and said in a strangled voice, "Sugar?"

He looked closely. In spite of the dejected air and her outlandish get-up, she had plenty to offer. She was small, with delicately turned wrists, a slender childish neck, an aristocratic little nose and a round stubborn chin. She looked about eighteen, he thought. A pushover for his talents. Eight-to-five he could clean up what ailed her in ten minutes.

"Thanks," he said. Then he went into his corny act, sensing that modern methods would be wasted here. "Excuse me for staring, but you're a dead ringer for my sister." He let his voice break a little. "We were pals."

She looked at him. It was an obvious effort but she did it. Score One.

"Were—?" she asked, emphasizing the tense.

He nodded gloomily.

"All over in thirty seconds. I always begged her not to drive so fast."

"I'm—sorry—"

"I'm not looking for pity." Her big gray eyes came to life. He saw he was on the beam. Something about the word pity got to her. "But she always came to me when she was in trouble—you look so much like her—it'd be like old times—" He passed her the ball and, as he expected, she ran with it. She said hesitantly, "I guess I'm in trouble, too."

"Boy friend take a powder?" She shook her head. He gave her a boyish grin. "Well, kid, if it's not love or murder, there's nothing a little dough can't cure."

He reached for his wallet and a fifty-dollar bill appeared on the table. She flushed and color improved her.

"Oh—please—" She pushed the bill back to him.

"Now, look. We're a couple of human beings, sitting two feet apart. One of us needs help. Why not chew it over and lick it together?"

"Thanks. I'm grateful but I—just can't talk about it."

"Sure you can. Like I always told Sis, pull it out in the open, it'll shrink like wool in hot water."

"But—why should an utter stranger—?"

"Kid, stranger's just an eight-letter word. What we are is two people with a problem on our hands."

He thought she was going to cry again, but she bit her lip and stayed dry.

"'Our'!" she echoed under her breath.

It was all over but the landing net. She made a small, tentative move toward the crumpled letter on the table. He reached for it, smoothed it out, and began to read:

March 4th

Dear Miss Jessie:

Please pardon my intrusion into your personal affairs, but both as your father's friend and his lawyer, I feel it my duty to inform you of the state of affairs here in Crawfey. For some months, your father's health has been failing but only lately I have ascertained that he is suffering from a malignant disease which can only have a fatal conclusion. I feel that your presence here, as his only relative and heir, is both desirable and necessary as promptly as your commitments on the Coast permit.

Your father is receiving all possible care and attention at the Cottage Hospital and the business is being run efficiently by Orville Bayne and the Standish boys. While the doctor gives your father a month or so, I am sure that you would wish to arrive in time to heal the breach which, unfortunately, exists between you and your father.

Hoping that this change of plans will not interfere too drastically with your picture career,

> I remain,
> Yours truly,
> Amos Fraser

Victor kept his eyes on the letter for a few minutes, digesting what he had read and drawing some shrewd inferences from it. The girl was one of the moths who had fluttered toward the arc light of Hollywood. She had not succeeded, as witness her shabby clothes and the dismal cafeteria. Her father's lawyer believed she was on the road to success. Therefore, she had been spinning fairytales to the folks back home. His lips twitched with amusement. Proud, unwilling to admit failure. Showed spirit. He liked that. It was what he would have done himself in her place. Next, he deduced that she came of solid stock, with a going business in the family which she would inherit shortly. It was probable, too, that she had come to Hollywood against her father's wishes, hence the clash between them. He gave her credit for nice feeling, reading her tears as signs of grief and remorse. He looked up and said: "Tough. But you mustn't take it too hard."

"It's not grief," she said, with reluctant honesty. "My father and I don't get along."

He laughed.

"You and me both," he said chummily. "I was so dead sick of having the Bible rammed down my throat as a kid, my draft-call was music to my ears."

She stared at him, a good deal of thought behind her eyes now. The impact of his personality seemed to hit her for the first time: the friendly blue eyes, the disarming boyish grin, the fresh vigorous maleness that flowed across to her like the spark between two arcs. She answered him slowly: "You were unhappy at home, too?" There was relief and responsiveness in her tone.

"Couldn't get away fast enough. And I never did go back." He bit his lip at the contradiction in his story but she hadn't noticed it.

"Well, I must," she said, with the sudden effect of coming out from behind her defenses.

"I get the picture," he said knowingly. "You came out to set the screen on fire. You flopped, but you told the home folks different: That letter says so. So now you're ashamed to go back."

"Oh, no. I've never been near a studio."

"Then why Hollywood?"

"To—to make my father sore. Hollywood's the closest thing to Sodom and Gomorrah I could think of."

"You sure hate him, don't you?"

"Yes, I guess I do."

"Why do you?"

Her little chin set stubbornly. She didn't answer. He could feel her freezing back into her former reserve. He didn't mind. He liked a pull on the line when he was fishing. What's more, the kid herself began to interest him. She was a different breed from the tramps he usually promoted.

"If you didn't go for pictures," he tried another angle, "what did you do?"

"Typing. In a wholesale plumbing business."

"So you're here in this crummy joint at 10:30 a.m.," he pointed out skeptically.

"I got a virus bug a month ago. They had to get somebody else."

"What you been using for money?"

"I don't *owe*—if that's what you mean," she flashed at him. "I *had* money—"

"I get it," he gibed. "Your dad staked you."

She answered with considerable dignity: "My grandmother left me a small legacy. As soon as I was twenty-one, I collected it and left home."

"How long ago was that?"

"Nearly a year."

He only half-believed her about her age. She looked more like a teen-ager than twenty-two. But the picture was coming clear, and it was right up his alley. Instead of an itching palm, he had a passion for handing out largesse. Here was somebody else who would remember Victor Clyde with admiration long after he had forgotten what she looked like.

"Open and shut," he smiled at her. "Lost your job, down to the cushion, then this letter, no plane fare and too proud to wire home for it. Right?" Her face told him how right. "Kid, you've got no problem at all." He gave the bill a push toward her. Then he paused. A much better idea occurred to him. He could do them both a favor. He put the bill back in his wallet. "Look. I'm driving east. I'm on my way right now. I can give you a hitch the whole way."

The color came into her face again. So she was straight. No casting couches or beach parties.

"Don't get me wrong," he said angrily. "This is no proposition."

His anger reassured her.

"But why should you—?" she began.

"It's a long ride," he shrugged. "Nice to have company." He didn't mention that her prim air of respectability made wonderful cover for him.

Traveling as half of an unexceptional-looking couple was as good as a disguise.

"But there are stops—and food—" she temporized.

He grinned.

"Hell, you won't always be broke. I'll keep score and you can pay me later."

All her defenses were down now. The careful reserve was gone and a vulnerable, insecure girl answered him: "I—didn't know there were people like—that."

The look in her eyes reminded him of that little tramp, Ruby, with the young brother at school. Bums or duchesses—and this kid had class—he could handle them all. He felt fine. But the urgency of his own position pressed upon him.

"Skip it," he said, pushing back his chair. "I'd like to get going. I'm due back east in a few days. How soon can you be ready?"

His matter-of-fact tone made the whole project natural. She gave a soft sigh of relief as she let him assume her burdens. She laughed suddenly, the first sign of lightheartedness he had seen in her.

"In about forty seconds," she said. "What I haven't pawned would rattle around in a teacup."

"Good. You live around here?"

"Two blocks."

"Let's go."

Her eyebrows rose at the impressive mauve-colored Cadillac, but she said nothing. Fifteen minutes later, he stowed her suitcase in the trunk beside his own handsome luggage and they were on their way.

CHAPTER FOUR

As soon as they were out of the city, he drove as fast as he dared. While he wanted no mix-ups with traffic police, he felt that the sooner he was out of California, the better. He doubted that Los Angeles would set up an eight-state alarm for a mere robbery, even with a bit of assault thrown in, but it was as well to get beyond the state line. As they streaked through the lovely fruit-laden valleys and then the flat reaches of the desert, he threw a glance now and then at the girl. She sat quietly beside him, making no attempt at conversation. But silence was a vacuum that Victor abhorred. Words, any words, were meant to fill it.

"What's your last name, Jessie?" he asked.

"Hewitt."

"Don't you want to know who I am?"

"You'll tell me when you're ready," she said placidly.

"I'm Victor Clyde." As she made no comment, he elaborated, trotting out one of his stock explanations: "I'm regional manager for a paperbox firm. Now they want me to take over the Eastern territory."

"Must be a good job. This is a car and a half."

"It sells boxes. Customers see it and figure I'm in the chips. So they get on the band-wagon."

"That's sound psychology."

He snorted inwardly. In spite of occasional attempts at the lingo he knew, she sounded like his elocution teacher back in Alma High. What had he let himself in for, teaming up for three or four days with an egghead?

"You teach school or something?" he asked suspiciously. It would account for her difference from the general run of girls, the clothes, the hair-do, the grafted-on slang which she must have picked up in Hollywood. A small-town school marm. . . .

"No," she answered, and volunteered nothing

further. It was like pulling teeth. But her composure amused and challenged him. He promised himself he'd know all there was to know about her before they reached Barstow. Nobody held out on Victor Clyde.

"What kind of a joint is this Crawfey?" he asked.

"You really want to know?" she asked diffidently.

"I'm asking, ain't I?"

She threw off her reticence and there was color in her voice as she warmed to her subject.

"It's the most conceited town in America."

"Conceited? How can a town be conceited?"

"It thinks it's better than the rest of the country."

"The whole town thinks so?"

"That's right."

"Why?"

"Well, they've got a funny history. They're all direct descendants of the early settlers. During the Revolution they sided with the British. They paid for it, too. After the war some of them went to prison, and the surrounding villages gave Crawfey a wide berth. They called it 'Torytown.'"

"So that makes it conceited?" he gibed.

"I guess I mean self-satisfied. They stuck together and ignored their neighbors. Everything British was fine, and everything modern was no good. Why, even today there's not a single TV set in the whole town."

"I don't believe it."

"It's true. For seven generations, they've been naming their kids Nigel and Derek and Basil—they still do. They hate change. Years ago the railroad proposed coming through Crawfey and making a big town of it. The village council voted thumbs down. They didn't want it big; they wanted it as is."

"Cockeyed. How do they live—take in each other's washing?"

"There's a whole crowd of commuters—we're only fifty-four miles from New York—advertising people, television executives, publishers—with enormous incomes—they live on estates and farms outside Crawfey. They just about support us."

"You mean taxes?"

"Well, that, too. But I meant jobs and trade. They've got this notion to raise asparagus and strawberries on week-ends—of course, they wouldn't know the first thing about it, so a lot of our boys have good-paying jobs, running things for them. Some of our women cater for them when they give dinners for each other, and our high school girls baby-sit for good stiff prices."

"And, of course, you soak 'em for groceries, et cetera," he commented dryly.

She shrugged. "Why not? We didn't ask them to come. The butcher, the barber, the liquor store—they all do nearly as well as my father."

"What's his business?"

"Hardware. He sells them disc harrows and power mowers by the dozen. And not knowing how to handle them, they're constantly going out of order. My father keeps the two Standish boys busy all year round just doing repairs."

"Nice for the Hewitts."

She turned to him shyly. "That's enough about the Hewitts. I'd rather talk about you."

It was a gambit he could never resist. As the car ate up the endless miles, he regaled her with tales, carefully edited and colorfully enriched; tales of war, in which Victor Clyde always got his man, and tales of peace, in which he surmounted all difficulties and vanquished all competitors. He had quite a smooth technique in pointing up his prowess. He belittled his own efforts and would finish, say, a skirmish with Japs, modestly:

" . . . it was a pipe. But those crazy kids in my battalion ran to our C.O. building me up for taking those Nips alone. Hell, I had a tommy gun, and there were only seven of 'em. I'm telling you, that D.S.O. they handed me was a steal."

Innocently, she ate it up. She sat sideways, devouring him with her eyes, her mouth a little open in rapt attention. She was an audience made to order for him and he enjoyed it to the full. By dusk, he was still talking and basking in her flattering absorption. They were deep in the Arizona desert. Now that they were out of California, his urgency had left him and the desert twilight was chill, even in the car.

He finished an anecdote and then said: "First decent place we come to, we better call it a day."

He heard her draw in her breath in a gasp. It took her a full ten seconds to find her voice.

"Whatever you say," she said steadily.

He suppressed a chuckle. So she was scared stiff, even if she hid it like a sport. Well, if she only knew it, she didn't have a thing to worry about. He had no intention of doing anything that could add up to trouble for himself. She was a pretty enough kid and he would have enjoyed a few hot passes, but it was too risky. One squawk out of her to the nearest sheriff, now that they had crossed a state line, and Victor Clyde's photo and fingerprints would be in the record, even if he beat the rap. No roll in the hay was worth that. And supposing she did no squawking (and from the looks she had given him, he thought she would be easy to persuade), it still worked out to grief. This Jessie Hewitt, of Crawfey, was a considerable cut above the casual intimacies of his world. Respectability stuck out all over her, in spite of the fact that she had allowed herself to be picked up and was taking terrific risks by throwing in with an utter stranger. He sensed that her background and bringing-up demanded permanence in any male-and-female relationship. And permanence was the one thing that Victor Clyde didn't want and couldn't afford. She was safe, all right.

When, a little later, they came to a neon-lighted motel near Flagstaff, he said, "This looks okay."

Again she answered, "Whatever you say." But, as she got out of the car, she was rigid with dread.

He set her mind at rest with a considerateness which cost him nothing, but which loomed enormous in her eyes. The proprietor offered a comfortable double room. Victor gave his disarming smile and said: "The wife claims I snore. Do you have two connecting singles?"

"I do, but it'll come to a little more."

"That's okay."

"Cabin M. Right at the end of the circle." He tendered two keys. "Light's on over the porch. Each room's got its own bath. Anything you need, there's a phone in every room."

"Right. Can we get breakfast in the morning?"

"From 6:30 on. I'd show you the rooms myself but I'm alone at the moment."

Victor paid for the rooms, then drove around the horseshoe that skirted the cabins, and parked before Cabin M.

"Go ahead and pick your room while I get the stuff out of the car," he told her.

When he came in with her suitcase and an overnight bag of his own, she was standing stiffly in the center of the farther room. He dropped her suitcase and turned away. Then he looked back over his shoulder and said matter-of-factly: "Better hit the hay. I'd like to get an early start in the morning."

She only nodded, but he ate up the look in her eyes. There was downright hero-worship in it.

CHAPTER FIVE

Although he was up early next morning, he found her dressed and sitting on the little porch, her packed suitcase beside her. As he hated waiting for anybody at any time, she went up another notch in his approval. After a good breakfast, they were on their way. The sun was still pleasantly cool, so he pressed a button on the dash and the top of the convertible folded back soundlessly.

"Get a little suntan or your folks won't believe you ever saw Hollywood."

She nodded and raised her head to catch the wind and sun. In five minutes, color whipped into her cheeks and little curls escaped the prison of her bun. She looked about fifteen, he thought, certainly not the twenty-two she claimed. He decided it might be fun to catch her out, and he began to probe: "Tell me about this legacy from your grandma."

"It wasn't very big. Just the hen-money she saved."

"Hen-money? I thought you ran a hardware store."

"We do—but we—" She looked at him with a deprecating smile. "It's a long story—I don't want to bore you."

"I'll tell you when I'm bored."

"Okay, then. There's always been a Hewitt's Farm and, until grandfather's day, it was big. But he hated farming. He was more interested in inventing things and monkeying with chemicals. He used to smell up the house so terribly that grandmother went on strike. Said she wouldn't cook anymore while everything tasted of sulphur and rotten eggs."

"So?"

"He built a workshop under the cellar with an outside ventilator to carry off the smells. Of course, that was long before I was born."

"I bet you and your friends had fun using it for a hidey-hole." All the life went out of her face. He wondered why but only said, "Keep going."

She recovered herself and went on but he noticed that she sheered away from the subject of her friends.

"Well, grandfather sold all but six acres to the Country Club for a golf course and opened the hardware store with some of the money. *I* think he did it so he could borrow whatever tools he needed for his inventions. He was a honey but a regular kid."

"His son didn't take after him?"

"No," she said shortly.

He dropped a friendly hand on her shoulder and took it away immediately.

"Look, Jessie," he said lightly. "Quit holding out on me. You got a thing about your dad. It sticks out every time you mention him."

"We just don't hit it off," she said stubbornly.

"Don't give me that. You come to Hollywood to spite him, you steer off the subject like he was poison, you don't give a hoot now he's dying. So you say you don't 'hit it off.' What kind of a cluck do you think I am to figure that covers it? Don't I rate the real dope?"

She tried her best to sound nonchalant.

"Haven't you had enough of my beefs? Finding me stranded and broke. Panhandling a ride. Can't you settle without East Lynne?"

"I'll settle for the whole works. Give, kid."

She was helpless in the face of his drive.

"All right, then," she said somberly. "We're like enemies. My mother died when I was born and I think he blames me for it. I read up all the psychology books I could find and that's the only way I can lay it out. He hates me. He loves to say 'no' to me."

" 'No' to what?"

"Everything. Parties, picnics, even having friends at the house."

"Don't tell me a smart kid like you couldn't cheat a little."

"I tried at first. Did things on the sly. It didn't pay."

"Guilty conscience?"

"Oh, no, he always found out."

"What's a bawling-out?"

He could hardly hear her answer, "It was—worse than that."

"Beat a little kid?"

"While grandfather was alive, he kept father in line. But since I was thirteen, we've been—alone. He really went to town on me then."

"You had neighbors, didn't you? You could have complained."

"And have them being sorry for me?" she snapped. "No, thanks."

He only half-believed her. Being an accomplished juggler with the truth himself, he could easily read her hard-luck story as a gimmick to gain sympathy and to graft a free ride across the country. And he had some foundation for his doubt. A kid who fed her folks back home fairy tales about her success in Hollywood could be trying the same stunt on him to make herself look interesting. Or maybe she was one of these pathological liars like that psychiatric guy in the Army used to yak about. Well, nobody got away with that stuff with him. A few smart questions and he'd nail her fast. It was a game he liked. He said skeptically: "So after he treats you like a dog all your life, the minute he gets sick, you burn up the road rushing back to hold his hand."

"I have no intention of holding his hand," she said calmly.

"Then why go back at all?"

"I'm the only Hewitt left," she said as if it explained everything.

"I see." He grinned insultingly. "Plenty of

pickings."

She took no offense. Instead, her face lit up with a forthright enjoyment.

"Oh, Vic, you're grand! I was scared to death you'd pity me and weep over me—but you treat me like I'm anybody—I don't have to worry if you're just being kind—"

Her tone, the whole screwy set-up began to convince him—and to bore him. He had little use for the imponderables. Besides, his own situation had brought up a new troubling question: racetrack characters followed the horses from meeting to meeting. At Santa Anita, he had seen many of the same faces he had seen at Hialeah, Belmont, and Atlantic City. Would this Herman Grotz, of the Hotel Mengo, come east after the California season was over? If he did, Victor's tidy little racket might well be shot . . . He answered Jessie absently and lost himself in his own affairs.

It was late when they stopped at a motel near Oklahoma City. Without even last night's facetious explanation, he asked for two rooms. If anything, the devotion in Jessie's eyes was deeper than the night before.

Victor went to sleep promptly. His restraint where Jessie was concerned bothered him very little. He liked a casual affair well enough, but his narcissistic self-love was far and away a stronger passion. He was taking no chances with Victor Clyde's safety and future for the sake of a dowdy little number who would probably be more grief than fun anyway.

Jessie lay awake much longer. The past thirty-six hours had been as violent as an earthquake. The whole landscape of her life had changed. For nearly ten years she had been about as miserable as a girl could be. Her father, puritanical and harsh, ruled Jessie with a heavy hand. And the hand often held a cat-o'-nine-tails to enforce his rigid code of duty and obedience. The girl had accepted, almost cheerfully, the burden of housekeeping, cooking, and helping out at the hardware store, wedged in after school hours. But service and submission were not enough to satisfy some sadistic strain in him. He took pleasure in denying her the normal companions and diversions of youth; he made a cat-and-mouse game of spying on her, phoning or even appearing at home at odd hours during the business day, to see that she was where he had ordered her to be. When she cheated, as she had confessed to Victor, Cyrus Hewitt was able to deal out punishment with a righteous feeling that his pleasure was also his duty.

To a certain extent Crawfey knew that Jessie was being raised with undue severity, but Crawfey minded its own business and respected a neighbor's privacy. The only manifestation was a show of kindness to Jessie herself. They meant well but she rejected their sympathy with a fierce pride which wrecked any chances of decent relationships. She spent her teens between a profound hatred of her father and a passionate refusal to make friends with people who might be merely sorry for her. Then, yesterday morning, Victor Clyde, personable, physically magnetic, and totally without any maddening pity for her, had elected himself her champion, her protector, her friend. Knowing nothing about her, asking nothing in return, he had solved her problems, made her decisions, and admitted her to a careless heart-warming fellowship. The glory of the facts filled her mind to the exclusion of everything else in the world. She lay awake, hugging the thought of Victor Clyde to herself like a suit of armor.

CHAPTER SIX

The rest of the trip was swift and uneventful. The status between them persisted. It required no effort for Victor to keep up his neutral attitude. Resistance was the prime motive force with him in any amatory adventure. And there was no resistance here. He was one hundred per cent sure that he could take Jessie with a single word or gesture and that fact robbed the situation of the spice that even a lightning affair should have. Moreover, Jessie's type was too alien to please him. Her outlandish clothes, her difference in background, and her unconscious disclosure of her feelings for him in every look, tended to cool any natural fire which the tempting situation provoked.

He felt kindly disposed to her in a mild way; anybody who admired him so whole-heartedly was entitled to his approval. And her personality, with its odd changes from childlike dependence on him to a quaint innate dignity at times, was refreshing enough to amuse him. But it would be no wrench to part with her when they reached New York. He would buy her a bus or train ticket to her little hole-in-the-ground and forget she ever existed.

On the last day of the trip, a minor repair to the Cadillac held them up in New Jersey, and it was late when he registered at the Commodore in New York. He took the usual two connecting rooms and a bellboy brought up all their luggage. As always, he tipped the boy lavishly and when he had left, carried Jessie's suitcase himself into the farther room. He said briskly, "Well, kid, this is the end of the line."

She turned dead white. "But—" she managed to whisper.

"It was a swell trip but it's over."

"You mean we won't ever—?"

"Better not, kid. Pickles and ice-cream don't mix."
She turned her back suddenly and stood, shoulders

drooping, head down, her small body somehow smaller, as if, ostrichlike, she could hide her feelings by shrinking in on herself.

Victor found himself at a loss. He could have handled tears easily, or even a hysterical outburst. But this silent puppy-dog misery tied his hands. If he attempted to console her, she would be all over him, sure that a kind word meant more than it said. He could, of course, brush her off with the cold-blooded truth: that he wanted no part of a dumb little cluck without even the know-how to use lipstick. But being Victor Clyde, he could not bear anybody—even a hick like Jessie—to think badly of him. Before the silence grew too long, the phone on the bed-table rang. The interruption relieved him enormously. He found he was beginning to sweat. Swiftly he picked up the receiver and listened, then spoke into the phone: "That's right, I did. No, thanks, I'll take care of it myself. Be right down." He hung up and turned to Jessie with a smile. "Forgot I was back in New York. I left the Caddy right out in front. I'll have to take it to a garage. Don't want any flip bellhop driving it even a block or two. You go to bed. I may be a little while." His hand went to his pocket. He took a few big bills off his roll and pressed them into her hand. "Look, kid. You say a day more or less don't matter about getting home. Buy yourself a nice outfit tomorrow and arrive in style. You don't want to look like a Hollywood flop when you greet the home folks." Without giving her time to answer, he moved to the door. "Got to run or I'll get a ticket. See you in the morning."

He found a garage and parked the car. Out on the street on foot, he breathed a deep sigh of satisfaction: he was home. New York at night; with a crisp tang in the March air. With its pink cloud cover, the reflection of a million city lights. There was nothing like it. He would walk a block or two, just to get the feel of it again—and to give Jessie time to cool off and get to sleep.

Her outburst had unsettled him, had even annoyed him. She was the kind of crazy mixed-up kid who might do something desperate, something that could involve Victor Clyde in unwanted publicity. Silly kids had been known to jump out of windows when they were crossed in love—then he grinned to himself. Hell, no girl with three hundred dollars in cash to spend on clothes would miss the chance of a Bergdorf spree. Probably right this minute she was making out lists of what to buy. He walked on, giving himself again to the unmixed pleasure of being home.

Naturally he gravitated toward Broadway, consciously savoring its unique essence: the gasoline fumes, the Hamburger Heavens, the soft-drink holes-in-the-wall, the nose-tickling soya of the chop suey restaurants. As he reached Times Square, there was an actual grin on his face.

The sight of the out-of-town-papers newsstand outside the Times Building gave him a thought. Maybe Jessie would like to read a L.A. paper once more before she buried herself in Crawfey. After all, she had lived there nearly a year. What's more, it might take her mind off him, keep her from deviling him, if she was still up when he got back. He crossed to the island and bought a Los Angeles paper.

As he walked away, folding the paper to fit his pocket, the front-page headline hit his eye:

POLICE CALL HOTEL MENGO
DEATH MURDER

He frowned. Hotel Mengo? Wasn't that the joint where his own last victim lived? So they had a murder there, too. He wasn't surprised, the place was a dump. He crossed the street and on an impulse, read the first lines of the article in the light of a shooting-gallery:

> An autopsy today on the body of Herman Grotz, veteran racetrack figure, determined that the cause of death was a skull fracture, sustained on March 7th, when Grotz, sixty-six, was the victim of a murderous assault during a holdup in his room at the Hotel Mengo.

Victor swallowed.

March 7th. Today was the 12th. He counted back. His attack on the elderly gambler had been on the 7th. He scanned the top of the newspaper. It was dated March 10th. A trickle of cold perspiration slid down his back. He looked around, crossed to a busy eating place, ordered the neon-advertised house-specialty, "ham 'n eggs," and unfolded the newspaper again. The article gave a resume of the holdup, Grotz's detailed description of Victor, and a scientific dissertation on the unusual "delayed action" between occurrence and effect of the deadly blow. Grotz had walked around for twenty-four hours with a fractured skull before he collapsed and died.

The next paragraph chilled him to ice:

> The police have connected the attack on Grotz with an earlier holdup in January on Lex Carver, cameraman of Colossal Studios, although, in Carver's case, no violence was employed. But in both robberies the use of a Hallowe'en mask and the description of the criminal point to the same hand. Moreover, the police have ascertained, through unnamed sources, that the same car was observed, standing for hours, in the neighborhood of the victim's home at the time of each crime. Described

as a lavender-colored Cadillac with out-of-state tags, witnesses dissent as to the exact state, although all agree that it was not a California license. An intensive tracer of all cars of this description is under way. The police are asking the co-operation of the public in reporting any such local car of which they have knowledge.

There was more concerning Grotz and police activities, but the print blurred before Victor's glazed eyes. Panic hit him. His legs turned to rubber and the green bile of nausea rose to his throat.

Murder. During the commission of a felony. No matter how unpremeditated, it was death in the gas chamber. What could he do? Where could he hide? Above all, how sever his connection with the damning Cadillac? After the newspaper appeal, Olsen, the superintendent of his Hollywood apartment, was bound to report Victor's car to the police, together with his suspiciously hurried departure the morning after the holdup. Thank the Lord he had said he was going to San Francisco. That gave him a short breathing-space if the police turned their attention north instead of east. Time enough perhaps to get rid of the Cadillac, change his name and lie low somewhere until the heat was off. . . .

Somewhere? Where? Where, in the whole United States, could he successfully dodge the police net which, in the course of a few days, would drop its entangling meshes over the country from coast to coast?

For the first time in his criminal career, he felt the huge drawback of working alone. There was no hide-out, no friendly underworld, no lawless organization to hold out a hand. The superintendent knew his face and name. It was just a matter of time when the clear trail of his flight east with its motel registrations would lead the police to New York. Where could he lose himself, where dodge the possibility of coming face to face with Olsen or, indeed, other tenants of the apartment house who could well know him by sight? Would the police import them to New York on the chance of putting the finger on him? A plane to Europe, Mexico or South America was the best answer, but that involved the delay and danger of the passport problem. And planes and ships would be watched. Better not attempt it. If there was some place where he could lie doggo for a month or two. . . .

He pushed back his chair with a clatter, dropped a bill on the table for his untouched "ham 'n eggs," and almost ran out of the place. Slowly he walked back to the hotel, working out the tricky details of his plan.

It was nearly midnight when he unlocked the door of his room. Lights were on in both rooms and Jessie was pacing up and down feverishly. As he entered, she turned and flew toward him.

"Oh, Vic! I thought you'd run out on me! I thought I'd never see you again—" She broke off and stared at him, frightened, and with reason. His face was still gray from shock and terror. "Vic! What's the matter? Where have you been?"

He sank onto his bed, cupped his face in his hands and began to put his project in motion. He spoke tensely: "Baby, I've been walking the streets, trying to come up with an answer."

"Answer? To what?"

"Us. I've been telling myself I've only known you five days all told. In another five I could forget you. But it's no good. I can't, honey—I can't give you up."

The change that came over Jessie was astonishing. The hackneyed comparisons which came to mind—a flower opening to full bloom, a sunrise lighting up a dark sky—conveyed nothing of the radiance that suddenly enveloped her. Her gaucherie and inexperience fell away. She seemed to grow sharper, more alive, and to sparkle with a gaiety and excitement that was contagious. She had come into her heritage—she was a woman beloved. She took sudden charge of the situation, her voice rich with joy and laughter.

"Give me up? Of course not. Why should you?"

"A million reasons. First, I'm ten years older than you—"

"What's that? Don't be ridiculous, darling."

"Our lives are too different—you from a place like Crawfey—and me, always on the go—it wouldn't work, I tell you."

She slid down beside him on the bed and threw an arm about his shoulder.

"Of course it'll work. I'll make it work," she said confidently.

"I know better. Give you a month back home again, you'll forget you ever knew me."

"You know better than that, Vic," she. said with absolute conviction. "We love each other. That's all that matters. I can handle the rest. We'll get married tomorrow and go home together."

"And be boycotted by your snooty Crawfey?"

Her laughter rippled. "For once, it pays to be a Hewitt. Crawfey will welcome you if you're married to me."

He dropped his eyes to hide his relief. Nothing to it. He could handle this hot little number as easy as putting a match to kindling. But he was not yet out of the woods.

"But, honey," he began tentatively, "it's only five days— you don't know a thing about me—"

"I know *you*. That's good enough." Her arm tightened. "Five days—it's been five lifetimes— Oh, darling, get it through your head—you're the only person in the world who ever really loved me or played fair with me—"

He had his cue. He gathered her close and kissed her thoroughly. Then he began on his second objective, the really ticklish one. But he had done a good job of planning on the way back to the hotel. With a kid as "sent" as Jessie, it ought to be a walkover. He laughed and said, "I'm not so sure about the playing fair. Baby, what if I told you I'd lied to you?"

"Lied?" Her tone was sharp with fear. "About what?"

"See? I told you. We'd never see eye to eye."

"What did you lie about?"

"My name."

"Your *name?*"

"Yeah. Victor Clyde's a guy who lived in my building in L.A. I just knew him to say hello to."

"But—why—?"

He turned to her and spoke reasonably and persuasively, "Get the picture, honey. I walked into that restaurant and there you are with a hard-luck story complete with letter and tears. I fall for it hard and offer to drive you east. You jump at it. Okay, we're on our way. Then, I begin to think. I start wondering if the whole thing's a plant, a gag to shake me down."

"To— How on earth—?"

"Jailbait."

"What's that?"

"Ever hear of the Mann Act? You start yelling bloody murder as soon as we cross the state line and I'm sunk—"

"As if I'd—!"

"I know, honey. I know, now. But I didn't, then. So when you asked me my name, I came up with the first one that popped into my head."

Her laughter rippled through the room.

"Is that all? Oh, Vic, how silly can you get? As if that could make a difference." She laughed again.

"What's your real name? And you'd better tell the truth this time because it's going on your marriage license."

He swept her into his arms and gave her another dizzying kiss. In his terror-stricken state, it was an effort. He hardly listened as she chattered on:

"Darling, I *will* go tomorrow and get a lovely new outfit. It's going to be so wonderful coming home—a marvelous new husband—" Her voice deepened. "I can face the whole town—I dare anyone to pity me now!"

"Forget that stuff, baby." There was a tinge of impatience in his tone. She sure had a thing about this pity stuff.

She straightened up, quick to catch the faint intonation of disapproval.

"You're right. I will forget it. We'll begin a brand new life. Mr. and Mrs.— Vic, what *is* your real name?"

He was ready for her.

"William Chase."

"Chase. That's a good New England name."

"The funny part is—my middle name actually is Victor. You can go right on calling me Vic."

He knew he was a little reckless, but he loved the name Victor—it seemed to describe him so completely.

"Mrs. William Victor Chase." She savored the syllables. He put a teasing finger under her chin.

"Jessie Hewitt Chase," he ordered, "go to bed and get some sleep. Tomorrow's your wedding day."

She clung to him.

"Vic," she whispered, "I'll stay if you want—"

He was in no mood to handle an amorous encounter.

"Nix," he said lightly. "The Chases only marry virgins." He turned her toward her room, gave her a smart spank on her bottom and pushed her to her door.

In bed, in the dark, his mind seethed. He was terrified as he had never been before in his life. He shied at the word murder, yet here he was, tagged and hunted as the blackest kind of killer. He told himself almost indignantly that he had only tapped Grotz with the gun; the guy must have had a skull like an eggshell. How was he to know that? It was just hard luck.

He gave his concentrated attention to the set-up with Jessie. Marrying her—marrying anybody—was utterly foreign to him but it had its points now. He would slide into place as Jessie Hewitt's husband in the God-forsaken little hole-in-the-ground Crawfey for as long as he considered necessary. When he felt it was safe to light out, marriage vows wouldn't stop him. Tough on Jessie, maybe, but God knows, she was asking for it. The kid was really "sent." (In the midst of his disquietude, a faint smirk curved his lips.)

He turned his attention to the immediate future, to tomorrow, when a dozen first-things-first had to be taken care of. The Cadillac, blood tests before he could get a marriage license, the license itself, an engagement ring for Jessie, and, of course, a wedding ring. Cash was no problem at present. He had enough in his money-belt for a long idle spell.

He wished frantically that the next few days were over. New York, so attractive a few hours ago, was now a deadly menace. At any turn he could come face to face with some California character, imported to point the finger at him. If he were only buried already in Crawfey. But could he believe Jessie's improbable tales of its ingrown isolation? How could any village, fifty-four miles from New York, shut itself away from the world, as she claimed? Should he forget the whole crazy maneuver?—should he get up and dress—sneak out of the hotel and run? He sat up and threw back the covers. . . .

Run? Run where?

No. Crawfey was his one and only bet.

CHAPTER SEVEN

Over breakfast, in Victor's room, he outlined the day's program to Jessie.

"A quick visit to a doctor for blood tests. Then you go shopping and I report to my office, downtown. That'll take me a good while, so take your time. If your cash runs out, send the stuff C.O.D. here."

"I'll never spend what you gave me." She smiled. "I only need one good-looking outfit to arrive in. No sense in getting fancy clothes for Crawfey. They'd be wasted," she said practically.

"I thought you wanted to impress 'em."

"No, I just want to come home in style to back up the stories I told." She giggled. "We're a fine pair of liars. Me, about my career, you, about your name—"

He laughed and squeezed her hand.

"Birds of a feather, honey. We'll get along like a house afire."

They found a doctor in the neighborhood who took the tests. In spite of Victor's urging, the doctor would not promise the reports under forty-eight hours. After that, Victor put Jessie on a Fifth Avenue bus bound for Fifty-seventh Street and hurried away to the garage for the Cadillac.

He drove to a large used-car lot that he had once passed on the Merrick Road on Long Island. There he told a plausible story about being transferred to the Far East by the oil company for which he worked. He accepted the dealer's first offer and while he took a substantial loss on the car, he was so relieved to be rid of it that he had no regrets.

Next he went to the Motor Vehicle Bureau on

Worth Street and applied for a driver's test in the name of William V. Chase, giving Hewitt's Farm as his address. He was told he would be notified as to the date of the test. (If Jessie got to the mail first during the next week and asked questions, he was sure he could satisfy her by some credible story about out-of-state licenses being only temporarily valid in New York). A much more ticklish matter was to keep her from seeing his present license, which he had held for years in his actual name of Francis Edwards. He would breathe a sigh of relief when he had an innocent new license and could destroy the old one.

From Worth Street, he took the Broadway subway north to the end of the line. At Van Cortlandt, he took a bus to Yonkers, alighted at Getty's Square and consulted a classified phone book in a drugstore, looking for a used-car dealer. An hour later, he was driving back to New York in a good-looking but conservative black Buick coupé, with a bill of sale made out to William V. Chase. The two transactions still left him a few hundred dollars to the good. He left the Buick in a parking lot and set out on foot to a Broadway jeweler's where he bought a two-carat solitaire ring (of less than blue-white purity but effective enough) and a platinum hoop, set with tiny diamonds all round.

For the moment there was nothing more he could do and he was increasingly nervous about showing himself in the New York streets. He went back to the hotel and arrived at his room with the sensation of reaching a refuge. Jessie was not yet back. Locking the door, he unfastened his money-belt and took stock. Even with the expenses of the trip east, the two car deals, the rings and the money he had given Jessie, he still had twenty-odd thousand dollars left. He transferred a couple of thousand to his wallet and refastened the belt. Money, at least, was no problem for a good long time to come.

At a quarter to six, Jessie knocked at the door. As he let her in, he stared. She was altogether charming. She had on a smart black suit and an intriguing Kelly-green hat. Her shoes and purse were green alligator and her three-quarter gloves were green suede. She had been to a beauty salon and her bright hair framed her face in the latest styling. The bedraggled kid of the Los Angeles restaurant—even the fairly attractively dressed girl of the second day of their trip—was gone. Here was a delightful, poised, desirable little dish, worth a second glance anywhere. Victor's sluggish pulse beat faster. This marriage business might have its points aside from its main objective.

"Like me?" she asked, rippling with laughter.

"Nope," he said, deadpan.

"What's wrong?" she asked, her eyes clouding.

"What you need is one of those cape things—what do they call 'em—?"

"Stoles?"

"Yeah stoles. Mink. Light-colored—you know?"

"Pastel," she breathed. "I saw one today." Then she flung herself at him, regardless of her finery. "Oh, Vic," she chuckled. "We'll have Crawfey goggling—minks and Cadillacs—"

He snapped at his chance. "I was just thinking, baby—maybe we shouldn't knock 'em so dead—get their backs up—"

"Something in that," she said, thoughtfully. Then she laughed. "Well, I won't give up the mink. So you'd better get a nice conservative paint job on the Cadillac."

"Right. I'll fix it up tomorrow."

"Oh—but your job—how can you?"

He caught himself up and grinned at her.

"Good news. I told 'em at the office I was getting married and the boss broke down and gave me a month's vacation before I take over the new territory."

"Oh, perfect. What a wonderful world."

He eyed her meditatively. Bad lot as he was, he still wondered at this slip of a girl who shrugged off the knowledge of her father's horrible disease and certain death without a word of pity or regret. For an instant her callousness chilled him. Then an unwilling grin parted his lips. Hell, he thought, she's like me. Knows what she wants and grabs it. And wastes no time lying about things she don't give a damn about. The old man was lousy to her so she hates him, sick or well. And she's got too much guts to pretend different. More power to her.

They dined early and spent the evening at Radio City Music Hall. Jessie, her head on his shoulder and her hand in his, was utterly happy. Victor, fretting at the delay before he could sink into the blessed security of Crawfey, could hardly sit still. Always before, at the first hint of danger, he had raced out of town, enjoying the thwarting of his pursuers and the novelty of his new environment. This waiting took more out of his nerves than any holdup he had ever attempted.

The next day, broken by the shopping for the mink stole, finally came to an end. On the following morning they picked up the blood-test reports, took the subway down to City Hall, and got their marriage license. An hour later, in a ceremony which shocked Jessie by its brevity and baldness, they were pronounced man and wife.

After lunch, at which Victor insisted on celebrating with a bottle of champagne, they went back to the Commodore to pack and check out. While Jessie superintended the taking down of their luggage by a bellboy, Victor brought the car around. At sight of the Buick, Jessie stared. "But Vic—where's the Cadillac?"

He laughed teasingly. "Didn't you tell me the

natives would hoot at a flashy car like the Caddy? Honey, I want your home-folks to like me. And the Caddy'd put two strikes on me from the go-off. So I turned it in for something quiet and respectable."

Her eyes filled with tears but she batted them away valiantly and trotted out one of his favorite locutions: "Oh, Vic! You're the most!"

He agreed.

CHAPTER EIGHT

They took the West Side Highway, turned off at Jessie's direction, turned off again and yet again on secondary macadam roads which bore northeast away from the Hudson. There was so little traffic here and the landscape was so peacefully pastoral that Victor could hardly believe the speedometer, which registered only fifty miles from New York. They began to pass estates, defined and sequestered by gray stone walls with iron gates. After a few miles of this, the undulating green reaches of a well-kept golf course spread out before them.

Jessie said, "Slow down. We're getting warm. Turn right into the next gate you come to."

The gateposts were old and weather-worn, and as Victor drove through them, he noticed that the road leading back to Jessie's house was a bumpy dirt road instead of the smart blue-stone driveways of the estates and villas they had passed. It was March, of course, the tail-end of the winter, but there was an air of neglect, even desolation, to the property, in sharp contrast to the trim tailoring of the golf course, glimpses of which could still be seen through a tall stand of trees to their right. Victor took a quick glance to the left and saw that there, too, Hewitt's Farm was cut off from view by a screen of imposing old trees. He caught glimpses of a handsome high-school building, set in ample grounds on that side.

The dirt road sloped gently downward and at the lowest point of the premises, a small, sturdy stone house stood, seeming to nestle like a cup in a saucer. To Victor, seeking isolation and concealment; the six acres, the solid little house, the surrounding cordon of trees, the whole situation itself, could not have been improved on.

In spite of the long unkempt grass in which it stood, the house had an air of classic simplicity. There was beauty in its clean virile lines. It could have been built in any era and looked as if it would stand forever. Jessie said, "Satisfying, isn't it?"

"Sure is. Don't see how you ever could leave it."

She answered with sudden hardness: "Were you ever beaten with a razor-strop when you were eighteen?"

He pulled her close, moved by his usual facile pity. "Why, you poor kid—"

"It was hateful. Well, that's all past. He's got pain enough, I guess, without our bad thoughts." Her tone changed with her usual mercurial speed. "Boy! Do we have work to do! The house'll be dusty—no food— you'll have to start the furnace—first honeymoon I ever heard of where the bride and groom had to clean up the love nest."

He parked before the house and Jessie surprisingly produced a key. Even if he had dreamed of anything as ardent as lifting her over the threshold, he would have had no chance. She darted into the semi-dark interior, pulling up window-blinds, dragging off dust-covers and opening doors like a brisk housewife.

To Victor, the house looked immaculate and comfortable. The furniture was old but it had been first-rate of its kind and it still was. The mahogany sideboard in the dining room might be of unfashionable bulkiness but when Jessie whisked off its dust-cover, it gleamed with a ruddy jewel-like sheen. There were only three rooms on the ground floor but they were all of good size and gracious proportions. The airy kitchen, hung with the warm glow of copper pots and pans, struck a note of contrast in Victor's mind. For the first time in years, he threw a thought to the ugly cheerless kitchen of his father's Ohio farm. The chill memory gave added bloom to his present surroundings. For an appreciable moment, he forgot that he was a murderer diving for cover; he felt as if he had come home.

He brought in their luggage and took it upstairs. The three bedrooms carried the same air of basic good taste. Everything was old but nothing was spurious.

The whole setup gave Victor a sharp feeling of importance; a sense of roots, of proprietorship. He was master here, owner of something solid, established, aggrandizing. It had a kick to it almost as exhilarating as those moments when he held a gun on a victim. A new sureness came into his voice:

"Get yourself unpacked while I tackle the furnace. Fix the beds and make a list of food we need and I'll run into the village. How far is it?"

"A mile and a bit. But, Vic, hadn't I better go, too, and call in at the Cottage Hospital?"

"Yes, I guess you should. But I'll start the furnace before we go. Be nice to come back to a warm—" he hesitated for a choice of words—"home," he finished.

They drove the "mile and a bit" to the village half an hour later. To Victor, it was something he had never before encountered. Some early colonist or builder had been hipped on Elizabethan architecture, and Main Street was a procession of dark-timbered houses with black vertical beams striping their upper stories. The only concession to modernity was that their steep roofs were slate instead of thatch. Most of these quaint, demure little houses held shops: a butcher, a grocer, a post office, all with living quarters upstairs. Larger than most was the hardware store marked "Hewitt's," with two broad show windows instead of one. The sign on the drugstore said "Apothecary," and there was no supermarket. It was a marvel that there was a movie theater.

At the far end of the village, on a tree-lined cross-street, a spacious frame house had been converted into a hospital.

"Come in with me," Jessie said. "Esther Wells is on the desk. If she approves of you, you're home."

Introduced to a stringy woman of forty, Victor was careful to leave the talking to Jessie, and behaved with a modest dignity, foreign to his usual brash personality. It was an effort but his life depended on his assuming the protective coloring of his surroundings and merging unnoticeably into this backwater—at least, for the time being. His boyhood farm bringing-up helped to make this easy; and where his safety was concerned, he stifled his urge to shine.

While Jessie went up to see her father, he listened to Esther Wells with a flattering interest, controlling his own itch for the limelight. He recognized her type: talking was to Esther what liquor was to some people, an outlet and an escape. With an inward smirk he could see her hard shell slowly softening up. Crawfey might be Crawfey but women were women. And, up to the age of ninety, pushovers for Victor Clyde.

When Jessie came down, sobered at her sight of imminent death, Esther said with rough sympathy, "No need to take on, Jess. We all know you've no cause to be soft about him, for all you kept it to yourself."

Even a week ago all Jessie's hackles would have risen at the idea of such sympathy. Victor had changed all that. She answered composedly, "What a fool I was—always pushing away the hands that were held out!"

Esther's eyebrows went up.

"I'll say this: you've grown up a good bit in a year." And something resembling a smile cracked her dour face.

"I can thank Victor for that."

"I thought maybe being a big gun in Hollywood did it," Esther said dryly.

Jessie grinned, looking like a boy caught breaking a window.

"That was a pack of lies, Esther, to save my face. The only good thing that happened to me in Hollywood was meeting Vic."

Esther's smile widened. She loved being in the know.

"Well, keep that to yourself, you gump. No need letting all Crawfey know. Go along now. You must have plenty to do. Your house has been shut up for two months. The dust must be an inch thick. And you've got to get the furnace started—"

"Oh, Vic did that when we dropped our luggage."

That did it. So this nice-looking well-dressed outsider was no mere figurehead. Victor was in. Esther pronounced the accolade: "Why don't the two of you have supper with me?"

"Thanks just the same, but we have to tackle the job some time, so the sooner the better."

Back in the Buick, Victor said, "That was a dumb move, spilling about Hollywood."

"No," she replied placidly. "Now we've let Esther in on the ground floor, wild horses won't drag it out of her. And she'll spread it around that you come up to Crawfey standards."

He gave her a sidelong look. She had a new poise since the night he had said he loved her. There was a self-confidence and a radiance about her that gave her color and spirit. It occurred to him that his stopover in Crawfey might be lively as well as prudent.

Half an hour later, the car loaded with bags and

cartons, they returned to the little stone house. The unsure companion of his trip east vanished, as did the tense emotional girl of two nights ago. Jessie was suddenly a practical, competent housewife, going about her tasks with skilled ease. Victor saw that he was forgotten in this swift but orderly campaign, and wisely went outdoors. He glanced into the garage (née barn) and at the well-polished Dodge it contained. He investigated the tool-shed and his latent manual knack itched at the splendid array of tools: gear for household chores, for cabinet work, for tilling the soil. His respect for Hewitt's Hardware went up. Everything was the finest of its kind.

He traversed the six acres of land, noting with satisfaction that the deep fringe of old trees hemmed in the place like a wall. Privacy was insured, and approach on foot from any side could be seen from some window of the house. The only path for a car was by the rutted road he himself had used. Crawfey was a snug refuge and Hewitt's Farm a fort within a fort.

With a farmer's eye he scanned the sloping land around the house. He surprised himself with a pleasurable resolve to plow up a couple of acres and start a miniature truck farm. It would soon be April, just the time to begin. He would clear the tall grass from the front of the house and lay out a flower garden for Jessie. The stalking and hold up of racetrack victims seemed suddenly as remote as China.

It was dusk when Jessie called him. He came into the cheery kitchen and sniffed a combination of delectable odors. With a serious and dedicated intentness, Jessie served him the best meal he had ever eaten, in a dining room made festive by good linen and candles in tall pewter holders. Afterwards she shoved him resolutely into the living room and cleared up alone. This new industrious Jessie amused him: Crawfey had stamped her again for its own.

He was hardly prepared for the next of her mercurial changes: when, at last, they retired, Jessie Hewitt Chase gave herself to him with the passion and abandon of a healthy pagan.

CHAPTER NINE

Four days later Jessie's father died. All Crawfey paid tribute to the name of Hewitt by its presence at the church and the graveside. There was solemnity but no mourning. Cyrus Hewitt had been as unloved by his neighbors as he was by his daughter.

Crawfey followed the immemorial usage of "calling" after a death. It was Victor's introduction and initiation. Within a week, he had met all of adult Crawfey and had come through the test with a passing mark. Esther Wells's vote in his favor had not hurt him, and Crawfey was also glad to do something at last for Jessie Hewitt without being rejected as they had been in the past. But Victor himself earned part of his welcome. He behaved with a nice blend of reserve and friendliness, feeling his way carefully and submerging his flamboyant personality until he felt himself on solid ground. After all it was his hide that was in danger.

He impressed Amos Fraser well and the lawyer himself suggested that Victor take over control of Hewitt's.

"Orville Bayne is an excellent manager," he said. "But any business needs a head. And Jessie is, after all, only a girl."

It was a ticklish assignment. For the last eight or ten months since Hewitt began to ail, Orville Bayne had been in virtual charge of the store. But Victor salved his pride by declaring his own ignorance of the business and listening to Orville as to an oracle. And the boy was indeed authoritative; he knew the business thoroughly and was unmistakably honest. In a week he shared all he knew with Victor, who was quick to grasp the various angles of hardware economy. He assured Orville of his continued position as manager and made only one major change: he decided to put in a line of electric refrigerators, washing-machines, air-conditioners, and television sets.

"What can we lose?" he asked the doubtful manager. "We need only buy one of each. We've got display room enough with those big show windows. If people buy, we fill our orders direct from the manufacturer. If they don't, we're only out the price of our exhibit."

"Maybe not even that," Orville replied, catching fire. "I might be able to get them on memo."

"Good enough," Victor laughed. "I said you've forgotten more than I'll ever know about this business."

Little by little Victor began to stand on his own feet. He was asked to go bowling and play poker with the men; he found himself slated to teach the Boys' Club boxing; and he and Jessie began to exchange visits with several young married couples. One thing he noticed: Crawfey might be sociable among its own, but it was not casual. Nobody "dropped in." There was always a phone call before a visit. Anything as informal as the borrowing of a cup of sugar at the back door was unheard of. There was a certain punctilio in Crawfey which was rigidly maintained. This reserve—was it the British inheritance Jessie had spoken of?—was distinctly welcome to Victor. He was asked few questions about his past and future activities. Vocal curiosity was at a minimum.

Not long after they were settled and were shaking down to a comfortably established position in the community, Victor did a little private research. He remembered Jessie's story about the workshop her grandfather had built under the cellar, and he had the criminal's instinct for a lair in time of trouble. A careful examination of the cellar finally revealed a barely noticeable square outline in a corner of the floor. It resembled a trap door but there was no ring or handle by which to raise it. Further examination was rewarding. Pressure on a certain spot caused the trap door to rise silently. He peered down at a short flight of steps. Intrigued, he brought a flashlight and descended. He found himself in a cozy underground room, part workshop, part study, decently furnished, even to a comfortable couch. There was a sink beside the workbench, and a tiny toilet in a compartment the size of a phone booth. The air was fresh and he remembered Jessie's mention of a ventilator. The whole setup surpassed his best hopes. In a pinch, here was an ideal priest's-hole if he should ever need to hide from the law.

He chalked up another point to Jessie's credit. This was a finer dowry than a million dollars would have been. The Victor Clyde luck again! Probably every house in Crawfey had its root-cellar, but Victor Clyde, as usual, went everybody one better. His house was tailored to his special needs. A man could stock the place with food and live, undetected and safe, till the heat was off. In a backwater like Crawfey, the contingency would probably never arise but it was a magnificent ace in the hole.

When his notice from the Motor Bureau arrived, designating a date for his driving test, and he told Jessie he was going into New York next day, she accepted it without question. Here again was another good mark for her: she was singularly free of nagging curiosity.

In fact life with Jessie wasn't bad at all. She adored him openly and lavishly (a satisfying state of affairs), but along with her devotion, there was a piquant independence of opinion where other people were concerned which had its attraction. She seemed afraid of nothing in the world—except losing him.

In New York, he took his test, passing, of course, with ease. He discovered that the weeks of safety in Crawfey had wrought a change in him. He was no longer fearful of showing himself in the streets. He had a new name, a solid identity and background. He felt he could parry any trouble that came his way. And he convinced himself that there would be no trouble. Even if Olsen, the Los Angeles superintendent, had reported Victor Clyde's departure, it would take long arduous work and improbable coincidence to connect William V. Chase of Crawfey, New York, with the murder of Herman Grotz.

It was more curiosity than apprehension that led him again to the Times Square newsstand which sold out-of-town papers. Over lunch, he scanned the Los Angeles paper from first page to last. There was no mention of Grotz, of mauve Cadillacs, of police activity of any kind that could interest Victor. The expression on his face was his usual smirk. As always he had outwitted his opponents.

But the smirk was overlaid by a sneaking discontent five minutes later. A stranger, seated at his table, finished his lunch and departed, leaving a New York *Daily News* behind him. As it lay on the table, Victor caught a glimpse of its date—April first— opening day at Jamaica. He could picture the cozy little track with its disproportionately large crowds, the eagerness of the bettors to throw their money into the machines after a tame, horseless winter. The pickings would be huge. And the thrill of pinpointing a particular victim, of trailing him home, of going skillfully about learning if he lived alone and was therefore eligible for Operation Hallowe'en—all this nagged at Victor like a toothache.

Driving back to Crawfey, he told himself not to be a sucker. He had fallen on his feet in a soft spot. He had a lovely home, a wife who adored him, a good cook, a pleasant life, and, above all, safety. He had only to tell Jessie he had resigned from his New York job so that he could run Hewitt's and become a gentleman farmer on a small scale, and he was all set. It was the only thing to do—at least, for a good while to come. And if the nostalgic twinge fretted him, what was that compared to the horror of the gas chamber? He turned into the bumpy driveway, feeling very virtuous; a resolute husband, householder and villager.

Jessie, looking charming in a green-sprigged housedress, served her usual good dinner. She questioned him only casually about his trip, reported that she had used his absence for the start of her spring-cleaning, cleared away the dishes and then came into the living room where he was listening to the radio.

"Turn it off, Vic," she said. "I want to talk."

He complied, giving her his ready smile. "Any time, honey. Much rather listen to you."

Without a pause she said quietly, "Vic, you're a professional burglar, aren't you?"

CHAPTER TEN

None of the conventional things happened to him; not the jolt like an uppercut or the chill down the spine or the feeling of having swallowed an ice-cube. He felt neither terror nor anger. This development was unexpected, but where Jessie was concerned, he now felt himself master of any situation. Her infatuation was a sharp sword in his hand. But native caution was, as usual, strong in him: why admit anything, even to this girl whom he could twist as he pleased? He answered her easily, "Very interesting. Where do you get that bright idea?"

"Don't think I was snooping," she replied defensively. "I began with the bedroom this morning and decided to put the small things away in mothballs—you know—wool socks, mufflers, sweaters—so I went through my bureau and your chiffonier. One of the chiffonier drawers was locked but of course the bureau key opened it. There was a little zippered bag. I thought it might have bathing trunks in it so I opened it. It held a pair of coveralls, a Hallowe'en mask, and a gun."

"So that makes me a thief," he said mildly. "That's one hell of a conclusion to jump to. Those things spell a masquerade outfit to my thinking."

"There was a box of Band-Aids."

"So?"

"Look, Vic. I was in Los Angeles a few months ago, too. I read about this man from Colossal Studios who was held up in his home. It was quite a colorful story—"

"I remember it myself." She was too warm for comfort. She might be nuts about him but she could still think straight. He began to do some fast thinking himself.

"The man wore Band-Aids on all ten fingers—" she went on.

"Right. The papers called him the Band-Aid Bandit, didn't they?"

"What made the story interesting to me was the thief's decency." She stole a look at him, half dread, half apology.

"*Decency?*"

"Yes. He delayed his departure long enough to look up a phone number in this man's—what's his name—?"

"Carver, wasn't it?"

"Yes, Carver's address book. And went to the

trouble of phoning him to go and release his friend as soon as he himself was safely away." She hurried on anxiously, as if to forestall his anger. "Look, Vic, to me stealing's not the worst crime in the Decalogue. I think cruelty to kids, meanness, tyranny—oh, a dozen things are a lot worse—"

"Is this a come-on for a confession?" he asked evenly.

"No. I really mean it."

"Well, skip it," he said in a bored tone. "It's not funny."

"I'm not trying to be funny. I just want the truth."

The truth. In spite of her big talk, she'd probably faint dead away at the truth. It was too risky. Let her have her suspicions but why hand her ammunition?

"You heard me," he said coldly. "Forget it."

She sprang up and spoke with sudden heat: "No, Vic! I tell you I don't care if it's true—nobody's perfect—"

"I said that's enough, Jessie," he said, and yawned deliberately.

"It isn't! I'm your wife. I love you. Not only your good qualities. All of you. The good parts and the bad parts. So don't shut me out!"

He stared at her for a long silent moment. His first thought was: at least, she doesn't know about Grotz. The papers had it the very morning I met her and she wasn't reading any news that day, she was reading only Amos Fraser's letter. So she doesn't know I hit him and she doesn't know he's dead. She's got me taped for some kind of a gentleman burglar—the Saint, or Robin Hood—Well, fine. If she's got these cockeyed ideas, the crazy mixed-up kid, maybe I can have my cake and eat it too. Crawfey's a swell cover for my racket. . . .

"Okay, Jessie," he said at last. "I won't shut you out." He lit a cigarette with a steady hand and spoke in a reasonable composed tone. "There was a guy in the Army always yakking about psychiatry. I could hand you a line, I guess. Hide behind that stuff—like childhood trauma causing conflicts in my subconscious. Well, I'm not going to. My childhood was as normal as buttermilk. And the war didn't split my personality, either. This thing is—well—physical—or—"

"Biological—"

"That's it. A question of—what do they call 'em?—hormones?"

"Genes."

"Righto. You're hep to that stuff, too. So you know these genes decide our makeup." He warmed to his subject. "A guy with certain genes has to be a musician if he starves at it— Another one with a different set of genes goes all out to be a doctor or bust— A third one can't be happy unless he's flying a plane, even when he knows the risk. Well, my genes are lined up in their own peculiar pattern. I get a charge out of matching my wits against the opposition. I like to plan an operation, study all the angles, then carry it out—"

"But that takes brains. You could be successful in straight business without the dreadful danger—"

He grinned at her. "The danger's part of it, honey. I guess my genes are organized something like the air-pilot's. He knows the danger, too—fog, wind, lightning—what's he riding but an over-sized tin cigar?"

"Planes are overhauled before they fly."

"Sure. They make flying as safe as they can. Same with me. I don't buzz out and snatch anybody's wallet. I plan a campaign, pinpoint my guy, study his routine, and case his home. I never make a move till I'm damned sure the risks are at a minimum. Then I—fly."

"But there's always the unexpected—the unforeseen—"

"That's the chance I take. I stake my freedom against the money I get. I earn it because I've got the courage to face the danger."

She had been listening to him with rapt attention, the moral issue in abeyance, as she hugged the fact to herself that at last he was admitting her to the crowning intimacy she hankered after.

But now, for a fleeting instant, all her Hewitt forebears sounded in the sudden repugnance in her tone: "Courage? When you carry a gun against unarmed people?"

The abrupt switch, the implied slur at his courage, infuriated him. That unruly second-self of his leaped up to take command, itching to do damage to this fool opposite him who dared to criticize. But his instinct for self-preservation was strong enough to subdue the murderous impulse. He needed Jessie and he needed Hewitt's Farm. Jessie was physically safe. But she knew too much. He would have to win her over, override her qualms and disparagement. And he hadn't a doubt in the world of his ability to do it. It took him a moment to bring his anger and his voice under control. Then he smiled and answered her glibly:

"Jessie, my gun is just a stage prop. It's true, it has a kind of psychological value. It keeps people from yelling. But I give you my solemn word that never— even in the tightest spot—have I ever fired it." This, being the literal truth, carried its own conviction. He gave her his quick charming grin. "Well, that's it, baby. You're married to a late-model Captain Kidd. Although I'll tell you this: I've never stolen a dime in my life that anybody earned. The people I've robbed all came by their cash without any effort on their part." (Conveniently, he ignored the Philadelphia car-dealer incident.)

"What on earth do you mean?"

He explained in words of one syllable the strategy

and execution of his racetrack program. He was stunned at her reaction: she laughed.

"Oh, Vic," she said, "it's an awful thing, but it has such a funny side. Those people, patting themselves on the back for their smartness, picking winners and going home loaded with illegitimate boodle, only to have somebody a little bit smarter take the wind out of their sails." To his relief, she came over and sat on the arm of his chair. "You know something? If ever there was such a thing as excusable crime, this is it. After all, if they'd lost their bets, nobody would accuse the mutuel machines of robbery."

His smug satisfaction at his easy victory was all but risible. But he was shrewd enough not to go on justifying himself. Instead, he deliberately began to blacken himself in order to jockey her into the position of defending him further. He said gloomily, "I ought to be shot for marrying you, baby. That really was a criminal act. I fought against it, but I just couldn't give you up. If you throw me out, even if you call up the nearest police station, it's coming to me."

"I'm not going to call the police, Vic."

"That's you all over, honey. But I couldn't blame you if you did. And it's no good saying I'm sorry. I wanted you, so I took a chance you'd never find out. Well, it didn't come off. If you're smart, you'll divorce me and forget me."

He turned and looked at her. Her eyes were wide with fear; not fear of his criminal practices, but fear of losing him. It was a swell weapon, he thought, and he would keep it sharp. He drew her close, exerting every ounce of his animal magnetism. She clung to him fiercely.

"Don't talk like that! You know I could never give you up!"

His answer was his mouth on hers, drugging her and robbing her of sense and sanity.

CHAPTER ELEVEN

Alone, thinking over this fantastic conversation, Victor felt intense dissatisfaction. Against his better judgment, he had for the first time confessed his mode of life, putting himself in another person's power. And that person, a crazy mixed-up kid with half-baked, teen-age notions; who today might condone, and tomorrow run screaming to the law that she was married to a thief.

Although he did not admit it—in fact, was not actually aware of it—it was partly vanity which had led him to be so expansive with Jessie. He was so sure of her that for once he had indulged his desire for an audience and his passion for applause. But sober second-thought restored his prudence. As things stood Jessie was a danger. So he decided that while she still looked on the rooking of a victim as an act of derring-do on his part, he must get her to participate in a job. Then if she changed her mind she could hardly sing to the police without involving herself.

He wasted no time. He proposed a delayed honeymoon in a spirit of high revelry.

"We'll stop at the best hotel in New York," he promised breezily. "And we'll paint the town like a rainbow. At night we'll hit the high spots and in the afternoons we'll try our luck at the track."

"You mean—look for a—a—"

"Sucker? We'll see." He rumpled her hair affectionately. "I can use a good lieutenant, at that." He felt how she tensed under his hand, divided between revulsion and desire for his approval. He gave her a little hug. "Nothing dangerous, baby. The ticklish parts are for yours truly. But there are certain things you could help with. Boy! Is this going to be a picnic—you and me on a job!"

He gave a plausible business excuse to Orville Bayne, and the next day he and Jessie drove down to

New York. He was as good as his word. Money was no object. They registered at the Waldorf—under an alias which he explained as necessary to avoid any linkage with Crawfey. He took her to the Stork, to Twenty One and other smart rendezvous. In the afternoons they went to the races and he was totally unprepared for the comic resultant development: Jessie became a violent horse fan. The crowds, the high-stepping thoroughbreds, the colorful jockey silks, and the recurring climax at the finish of each race intoxicated her. And she was not content to be a mere spectator; she wanted to bet. Victor laughed at her but supplied her with money. She concocted a "system" of her own (probably as effective as the much-touted ones) and didn't do badly. Her effervescence when she won a two-dollar bet marked her, among the people around her, as a typical novice. The dyed-in-the-wool bettors were rarely vocal during or after a race. They looked on her with a kind of tolerant amusement.

This suited Victor very well. It was useful protective coloring for him and his stalking. Any Pinkerton man who saw him with the amateurish Jessie would eliminate him as a menace without a second thought. Meantime he pursued his usual routine in sight of the fifty-dollar windows and by the fourth day had marked out a victim. He waylaid Jessie in the aisle on her way back from the cashier's window. "Look, honey, think you can find your way back to town by train?"

"Train? Why should I?" she asked.

"I've got to trail a guy."

Her flushed exultant face sobered. "Oh Vic! Must you?"

He frowned. "Answer me," he said shortly.

"I could, of course," she said with quick compliance. "But why can't I go with you?"

"You're too conspicuous."

"I?"

"It's no cinch trailing a guy in this mob. I may have to stick close so as not to lose him. And if he gets a few glimpses of the same pretty girl tagging him, he may get ideas—if not now, then afterwards."

She gave him a startled look; the abstract idea of Victor's racket might be excusable, but as a reality, in actual operation, it was frightening. He gave her no time to develop any jitters. He went on quickly to his real point: "The other night you were yakking 'Don't shut me out.' Was that just a line or did you mean it?"

"I—I meant it."

"Okay, then. I can use you."

"Use me?"

"Look," he said with curbed impatience, "are you in or out?"

"In," she said faintly.

"Then listen. There's a fifty-fifty chance the guy came out by train. In that case, you'll do the trailing." He was furious at the horror in her eyes.

"But I don't even know what he looks like," she temporized.

"I'll point him out to you in a couple of minutes. Keep your eye on him even if you have to give up your seat and stand in his aisle for the rest of the day. From the seventh race on, stick to him like a brother and if he does take the train, don't lose him. Be ready to walk, take a bus, or a taxi at Penn Station, but trail him home. Can you do that?"

She swallowed. "I—I—"

"I thought you were the kid who didn't think stealing was so bad—"

"Yes—but—"

"Great on the gab, but when the chips are down—yellow—"

"It isn't that—"

"Okay, forget it," he said curtly, not hiding the

contempt in his voice.

She reacted almost shrilly, "Yes, I can do it. Point him out!"

He warmed her with his smile. He squeezed her hand. "I knew I could count on you. And, baby, don't look so scared. Chances are he drove out and he's my meat. And if he does go by train—hell, honey, it's no crime to follow a guy. The New York streets are free."

After the eighth race, it became evident that Victor's quarry was going by train. With an air of nonchalance she was far from feeling, Jessie merged into the crowd behind him, so close that she was literally touching him. On the platform, the empty race-train was waiting. Without effort on her part, she was injected into the car by the force of the mob behind her. In the scramble she instinctively took a seat behind her victim and across the aisle, so that she was out of his line of vision. Standees all but cut off her view of him, but as the crowds shifted in the swaying train she managed to get a good look at his back and profile. His clothing looked expensive but too sharp for good taste. He was about forty, rather fat and soft-looking. She was sure he was the slothful type who would take a taxi for even a block or two, rather than walk. She began to worry about the mechanics of getting a second cab and keeping him in sight after they reached Manhattan. It seemed suddenly the most important thing in the world to come up to Victor's estimate of her; so important that it blacked out her squeamishness at the nature of the job and its criminal significance. At the same time, a second force was in operation, stifling her qualms and urging her on; a force rising from her subconscious mind like a jinni out of a bottle.

At Penn Station, her quarry did indeed take a taxi, one of a long line, parked at the ramp. Jessie, being immediately behind him, was able to get the next one.

As the door slammed, her driver shook all the sense out of her by three words: "Where to, lady?"

She had a horrible moment when speech deserted her utterly. It was the thought of Vic's frown if she failed him that finally forced the desperate words to her lips:

"Go wherever that taxi ahead goes. Don't lose it."

The driver took a swift glance over his shoulder at her. He saw a pale, tense but attractive kid sitting bolt upright. He grinned, sure that the kid's husband was in the taxi ahead. And he wondered what charmer the husband had in view to desert such a nifty little dish as his passenger. He shifted gears, muttering.

In the clotted traffic of home-going Manhattan, it was easy. Both taxis moved at a snail's pace and it would have been impossible for Jessie's driver to do anything but follow the first car, practically bumper to bumper. As they drove, Jessie's nervousness began to die. She was able to think and plan. She took several dollar bills from her bag and held them ready, so that she would not be delayed unduly at the journey's end.

She needed only one of them as the first taxi pulled in before the entrance to a large flashy hotel on Forty-eighth Street. She thrust the dollar at the driver and started to open the door. He chuckled and said, "Hold it, Sherlock. Give him a head-start or he'll get a gander at you and you'll never get the goods on him."

"Oh—yes—" she stammered, flushing. The driver was enjoying himself.

"I'll say when," he told her. "You keep under cover."

He watched the plump passenger of the first taxi step out and registered his amazement that the girl should consider such a character worth fighting for. The car ahead pulled away and the passenger turned toward the hotel entrance. Jessie's driver said, "Go to lady. And nail him where it hurts."

It proved almost too simple. As Jessie reached the desk, her quarry was saying, "Four-twelve."

And the desk clerk, as he handed out a key, inquired, "Have a good day, Mr. Pinelli?"

Jessie slipped away, left the lobby and took another taxi to the Waldorf. As she sat back, that strange second emotion rose again from her subconscious: an exultant triumph over her father. She had defied him effectively at last. She had just proved it by a lawless act. She was even sorry that her share in the projected holdup was so innocuous. A real crime was her best answer to Cyrus Hewitt's upbringing.

Victor, imperceptive though he was, had come close to the truth when he labeled her a "crazy mixed-up kid." If ever there was a ripe subject for psychiatry at the moment, it was Jessie. Her unhappy girlhood had bred a hatred of her father as sharp as a knife. It had dominated and warped her life. When she met Victor, she was a made-to-order victim for his crude tactics, ready to enlarge his smallest kindness into a glowing act of tenderness, to read his cagey agreement to separate rooms as a deed of high chivalry, and his casual gift of money to outfit her as princely generosity. Her gratitude, plus her physical feeling for him, was a combination guaranteed to muddle a far cooler head than hers. She was like a hot-rodder without brakes, hurtling downhill.

CHAPTER TWELVE

Victor was waiting for her when she reached the hotel. Inwardly, he was more nervous than he would admit. He feared some violent revulsion of feeling in Jessie which might have put her off the job he had set for her, and much worse, off him and all his works.

In the fifteen minutes before she came, he even had nightmare visions of her arriving with a policeman. The charming hotel room felt like a trap. His uneasiness led him to get his gun from his suitcase and drop it into his coat pocket. If she ratted on him, it would be her last act.

Her familiar long-short tap on the door was no proof that she was alone. Gingerly, he opened it with his left hand, his right one in his pocket. Instantly he knew that everything was all right. Jessie swaggered into the room with an air of brittle vivacity. If he had not known that she never drank, he would have thought her exhilaration came from a cocktail or two. He ran his tongue over his lips and asked as jauntily as he could, "Operation Bloodhound accomplished?"

"Oh, sure," she said airily. "Nothing to it."

"Good kid! Let's have it."

"Hotel Rogers. Room 412."

"Baby, you're a wonder!" He came toward her, his arms open.

"Don't you want to know his name?"

"His—!" He burst into a spontaneous shout of laughter. "Quit the kidding—"

"It's Pinelli," she said coolly. "Sorry I couldn't get the first name." As he swept her into his arms, she clung to him in a fever of passion, all her pertness gone.

"Vic—Vic—now you know how I love you!"

"You got nothing on me. Baby, you're a real doll."

Two days later, Mario Pinelli, a moderately important cog in a profitable narcotics ring, was relieved of seven thousand dollars in his room at the Hotel Rogers. Ordinarily he would have fought shy of calling in the police under any circumstances, but the situation got beyond his control. Being who he was, he went "heeled" and as the masked Victor confronted him, his hand went to his shoulder holster. The gun never became effective. Victor's sharp blow on the head reduced him to involuntary co-operation. Half an hour later a chambermaid found the unconscious man, rang the desk and thereby set in motion the machinery of the law.

Pinelli, cagey as all his kind, was monosyllabic, volunteering nothing except that his assailant was masked and wore adhesive tape on all his fingers. He was vague about the amount stolen and, for his own reasons, silent about the fact that the money was racetrack winnings. The holdup rated an entry on the police blotter and a half-inch squib in the tabloids.

But it was a milestone in the relationship between Victor and Jessie. Her actual participation in the job set his mind at rest. He was no longer at the mercy of her moods or scruples. They were partners. Like some twisted Pygmalion, he felt pride and a macabre enjoyment in having molded his crooked Galatea from such law-abiding material as Crawfey. Moreover, he now had an audience, a luxury he had missed for long lonely years. From all angles things could hardly be improved. The heat from the Grotz disaster was apparently off. He could come and go as he pleased. He could pull a job or two or three with the delightful security of using Crawfey as an invisible cloak in case of trouble.

Jessie clung to him with the grip of a drowning swimmer. She had only one desire: to identify herself with Victor, mentally, morally and physically. And the way to that was to be what Victor wanted. She felt an actual disappointment when their next quarry drove a car and she had no part even in the trailing operation. She softened this disappointment by taking on the job of staining Victor's Band-Aids flesh color with foundation cream, declaring pertly that this surely was her department. Victor also used her to do the preliminary phoning to ascertain if a prospective victim lived alone or not. When someone did answer the phone, as often happened, her cool handling of the situation won his approval. That was all that mattered.

Of course there were bad moments, moments when reality became a nightmare. No girl of Jessie's background and instincts could help, now and then, being suddenly engulfed in horror at the cold facts: she was the wife of a thief and equally a thief herself, aiding and abetting and living on stolen money. There were times, as she talked of church or garden affairs to Esther Wells or Maud Chiltern, when a wave of hysteria would break over her and she kept herself from lunatic laughter only by locking her jaws together.

But the thought of Victor was enough to kill her qualms, or at any rate push them so far down in her consciousness that they ceased to trouble her. It never occurred to her to ask Victor to give up his "profession." Instinctively she knew that he would not and (what was far more important) the request would weaken the bond between them. Little by little, she had come to know that oneness with Victor meant oneness in his point of view. And if it came to a choice between Victor and honesty, honesty hadn't a chance.

She lost all perspective in her desire to shine in his eyes. She talked of little else besides the "jobs" they lined up and would have hurried from one to another if it had not been for Victor's wiser moderation.

He insisted on periodic returns to Crawfey between operations, if only for a weekend, explaining carefully to Jessie the need to associate themselves with the local life and to account to their friends for their absences. By the end of May, most people in Crawfey gathered that Victor was regional manager for a large firm of paper-box makers. He was understood to travel through a dozen states, checking on district salesmen and holding conferences as he went. Jessie, having had the necessary training, went along to act as his secretary. It was neat and practically unassailable. Both he and Jessie reasoned that even if a Crawfeyite visited New York on a rare errand, both the big hotels and the racetrack would be out of his orbit.

Victor went out of his way to win Crawfey's confidence and liking. He spent money lavishly on sports paraphernalia for the Boys' Club to make up for his personal services which were naturally curtailed by his "business" absences. His donations to the Community Chest, other local charities and even the collection plate were extravagant. Jessie, with a better perspective on Crawfey, tried to deter him. "Darling, you mustn't. Giving so much attracts attention."

He gave his hearty infectious laugh.

"I like to attract attention, baby."

"But you shouldn't. You should just melt into the landscape. In Crawfey, it's not smart to be different."

He gave her a patronizing pat.

"Let me decide what's smart and what isn't," he said largely.

Instantly she was conciliatory. She spoke with voluble haste: "Oh, Vic, I'm not trying to— Of course you know. In New York you think of the cleverest things that would never occur to me. Like changing hotels, for instance. A week at this one and a week at that one, and always under different names. And keeping the car in a parking lot instead of a garage so you don't have to give your name. But—here—it's just—I thought—knowing Crawfey—"

This girl was almost unrecognizable as the Jessie Hewitt of a year ago who had the spirit to defy her father and leave home; or even the girl Victor had met less than three months ago. Not the greatest of Victor's crimes was robbery with violence.

CHAPTER THIRTEEN

The biggest job of Victor's life practically fell into his lap. It differed from all his other undertakings in that it was a spontaneous operation, done without any preliminary planning or trailing. It happened on Decoration Day, which is always a banner day at the New York tracks. The horses were running at Belmont and large as that lovely track is, by noon, when they arrived, the grandstand was packed solid. Unless they were willing to stand all afternoon, they had to go to the Clubhouse. To Victor, it meant a day lost, since he was leery of the smaller arena of the Clubhouse where his activities might be conspicuous. But he could afford to take the loss of a day philosophically, since he had "pulled" three successful jobs over the weeks for a total of seventeen thousand dollars. He would devote Decoration Day solely to Jessie's enjoyment and might even put up a few bets of his own to be sociable.

They were lucky enough to find seats in the third row and Jessie settled down busily to pick out two horses for a Daily Double. As this feat consists of selecting the winners of both the first and second races, out of the dozens of entries comprising the two contests, the remuneration is correspondingly high. Victor stayed beside her, not even attempting his usual prowling near the fifty-dollar windows behind the stand. He even enjoyed the novelty of attending the races as an amateur and went so far as to select a couple of Daily Doubles for himself, based on the top choices of the *Morning Telegraph's* pundits. Jessie had her own method: she used her age as her guide and played Number Two in each race since she was twenty-two years old.

When Number Two actually won the first race, she seethed with excitement. It was a long shot and regardless of who won the second race, the Double would pay a respectable sum. During the betting interval before the second race, there appeared on the odds-board the amount that each horse would pay, provided it won, coupled with Number Two in the first race. The combination Two-Two would pay two hundred and three dollars for a two-dollar ticket.

As the second-race horses went to the post, Jessie's excitement mounted to a fever. It was not the actual money but the thrill of picking the winners that stirred her. Or perhaps she threw herself into an artificial animation to still any latent scruples that refused to die. The race was at seven furlongs and at the break, the red silks of Catch-em-all, Number Two, were far back in the pack. Jessie groaned. But the Belmont track with its long stretch gives a horse with stamina plenty of opportunity to show its worth. Little by little, the aptly named Catch-em-all made up ground. At the eighth pole he was fourth and gaining on the tired pacemakers ahead of him. At the sixteenth pole, he was level with the leaders and at the wire, he swept over the line a clear length ahead.

There was an ungodly yell behind them. Practically everybody in their row of seats turned to see who had uttered it. A big laughing man was clutching a thick wad of tickets and shouting to a man in the next seat, "Woo-hoo! How's that for picking 'em? One hundred smackers on Two and Two!"

Jessie, sparkling and laughing, cried: "Me too! I won the Double, too."

"Good for you, sister," the man laughed back.

Victor took one quick glance at him. It was enough. He recognized him immediately, as would anybody across the whole country who owned a TV set. The hearty buoyant personality, the wide gay grin, the big loose-jointed figure were the sign and symbol of Lee Mack, one of the outstanding composers of popular music in America. Lee Mack's place was beside George Gershwin, Irving Berlin and Richard Rodgers. But what made him familiar to the public was his gift for dramatizing his own music at the piano with a leaven of entertaining patter thrown in. He was as well known to the viewers as Victor Borge or Liberace.

Victor knew even more about him. A few nights before he had happened to see an illustrated article in a slick magazine dealing with Mack's life. He would probably not have read it through (being no reader) except for one fact: at the head of the article there was a picture of Mack's soundproofed penthouse at the swank Hotel Cleveland, where he turned out his lilting melodies so inexhaustibly. Victor's eye and attention had been caught because he and Jessie were currently stopping at this same Cleveland Hotel, were, in fact, housed on the twenty-first floor, just two stories below the pictured domain of Lee Mack. A sense of identification, almost of kinship, made him read the article from end to end. He learned that Lee Mack had been born in Utah, was thirty-three years old, unmarried, a man who worked hard and played hard, who did his serious composing in the small hours before dawn (hence the special soundproofing) and many other miscellaneous facts.

And here was Lee Mack announcing to all and sundry that he had won fifty Daily Doubles of two hundred and three dollars each, an aggregate of more than ten thousand dollars.

Victor did some fast thinking. He let Jessie collect her winnings and even watch the third race before he said in an undertone: "Get your things together. We're leaving." As she opened her mouth in protest, his voice grated at her, "Don't argue."

She bowed to the finality in his tone and nodded without argument. But as they drove back to town, she turned to him worriedly.

"Vic, tell me. Was there someone who recognized

you—someone you've got to dodge?"

"Nothing like that." He smiled.

"Then why—? It can't be a job—we haven't been checking on anyone."

"You're going to do that in a little while."

"Who is it?"

"Wait and see."

"Don't be so mysterious. I've got a right to know, haven't I?"

"You sure have, honey. All in good time. But you'll do your stuff better if you don't know names and places until later. Now here's the setup. When we get to town, I'll give you a number to call from a drugstore. If anyone answers, ask for Mrs. Smith—Jones—anybody— Hell, baby, I don't have to coach you. You've done it often enough. If there's no answer, the deal's on. I'll park the car somewhere near—the streets'll be empty on a holiday afternoon—and we'll walk to the hotel. When we get there, we tell the desk we're checking out, pay our bill and go upstairs. You'll pack our stuff while I . . . see a man about a bankroll. When I get back to our room, we phone for a bellboy to take our luggage down and we're out of there before there's a peep out of our target. Simple?"

"Routine," she agreed with a show of blasé coolness. So what's all the secrecy for?"

He reached over and chucked her under the chin.

"Anyone ever tell you you're the picture of respectability? That's a big asset to the team, baby. I wouldn't want to spoil it by guilty knowledge. Oh, one thing more. Think you can hide the zippered bag while we go through the lobby?"

"Of course. I'll carry my mink stole over my arm with the bag under it."

"Fine. I never made a better buy."

In Manhattan they stopped at a drugstore and he looked up Lee Mack in the phone book. Unlike some celebrities, Mack had no fixed idea about privacy which might have manifested itself by an unlisted number. Victor went over to Jessie and said, "Okay. Call Chapman 3-6020. And let it ring plenty."

She let it ring eleven times before she hung up. "No answer," she reported.

"Here we go," he said, the excitement of action and danger coloring his voice.

They carried out his preliminary plans without a hitch. At half past four, up in their room, Victor picked up the zippered bag.

"You've got duplicate keys to the car," he said. "If I'm not back by 8 p.m. you'd better vamoose and get back to Crawfey. They'll want the room. I can always get a bus to Pound Ridge. I'll call you from there and you can pick me up."

"If I have to get out of the room, I'll wait in the car," she said firmly. "No matter how late you are."

"If that's how you want it," he shrugged.

There was a touch of hysteria in her answer: "Yes, that's how I want it! I want to be with you every step of the way. You know that."

"Right, baby," he said, kissing her. "Be seeing you."

Carrying the zippered bag, Victor, after a glance up and down the corridor, made his way toward a door with a red light over it. He thanked his stars that his room was on a cross corridor, out of sight of the floor-clerk's desk. He opened the fire door and found himself on a flight of stone stairs. He stood still and listened. It was as silent as a tomb. Carefully, with hardly a sound, he mounted two flights, opened the door a crack and peered through.

The layout of the twenty-third floor was different from the lower ones. Here only four doors opened onto a central corridor. Victor cursed under his breath. So there were four penthouses and he had no idea which belonged to Lee Mack. He stole out into the corridor and gave a swift look around but no door bore an identifying card or name-plate. He could not dare enter any penthouse at random. That was asking for trouble. He did not do business in that haphazard way.

In a fury of balked achievement, he decided to abandon the project. He turned back to the emergency door. As he did so, his eye caught a touch of dull color on the floor before one of the doors. He tiptoed over. It was the manila wrapper of a magazine, lying on a doormat. He bent closer. It was a copy of *Musical America*, addressed to Lee Mack.

With a chuckle of triumph, all his daring resurged. But he was still cautious. It was nearly an hour since Jessie's phone call to Mack's apartment. He would test again. He rang the bell, waiting, tense but ready with a glib lie in case someone came to the door.

No one came.

Victor slipped his trustworthy bit of celluloid out of his pocket and went to work on the door. In a matter of seconds, he was inside, leaning against the door, waiting until his harsh rapid breathing slowed to normal.

After a few moments, master of himself again, he made a silent tour of the penthouse. It was a revelation to him. The living room or studio, as the magazine article had called it, was at least forty feet square. An immense concert grand piano stood before a tremendous picture window which framed a sweeping view of Central Park. The room was so big that without crowding there were two huge semicircular couches, easy chairs, tables, a monster TV set, radio and record-player and a vast desk spread with handwritten sheets of music. There was a mammoth fireplace and on the mantel above it stood half a dozen exquisite small figures of animals, wrought in pure gold.

Victor stared in wonder but not in envy: he had no

use for anything but unidentifiable hard cash. Nor in the bedroom did the evidences of careless luxury tempt him. In an unlocked casket on the dressing-table lay a clutter of diamond studs, platinum cuff-links and gold tie-clips. He touched none of them.

After a thorough survey, he opened the zippered bag and began his routine. As he stuck on the flesh-colored Band-Aids, he cast a fleeting smile two floors down to Jessie who had so diligently tinted them. A good kid, he thought, and surely gone where he was concerned. It was a novelty—and a nice one—to own and control another human being, especially one with Jessie's good qualities. She was pretty, quick in the uptake, and above all, owned Hewitt's Farm which was Victor's ace in the hole when trouble threatened.

He slipped on his coveralls, adjusted his Hallowe'en mask and transferred his gun, adhesive tape and other paraphernalia to his pockets. He was sure he had plenty of time because the races would be over later than usual, due to the crowds. Traffic from the track to Manhattan would be very slow. Still, it was possible that Mack would leave before the last race to avoid the traffic tangle and arrive earlier than expected. Well, he was ready.

Suddenly a question assailed him: would Mack be alone? He cast his mind back to that boisterous moment after the second race when Mack had announced his winnings. Had he announced them to the world at large? Was the man next to him a friend or a mere ear for Mack's exuberance? Everybody spoke to his neighbor at the track in moments of excitement. Mack had probably done just that. But if the man had been a friend and did arrive with him shortly . . . Well, a gun was a great equalizer. Victor had proved that he could handle two men when he pulled the Philadelphia job. Nothing to worry about.

He selected a clothes closet as large as a small room for his hiding place and waited in a chair in the bedroom for the sound of Mack's key in the lock. His mask was hot and uncomfortable but Victor sat with the stony patience of a cat at a mouse hole.

It was about half past six when the front door opened. Before it had slammed shut, Victor was in the closet, his eye to a crack in the nearly shut door. Mack strode into the bedroom, singing one of his own songs at the top of his lungs. He shed his coat and shirt and made his way to the luxurious bathroom with its green marble washstand, its nine-foot tub and its shower stall studded with spray fixtures in all four corners. Victor tiptoed to the bathroom door, his gun out.

"Reach, brother. This is a stickup."

He was totally unprepared for his victim's lightning reflex. Mack whirled and lunged. A tremendous clip on the jaw sent Victor reeling back. He stumbled into the bedroom and clutched at a chair. Only the plastic mask saved him from unconsciousness. Mack dashed past him toward the studio and the front door. Sagging on his knees, Victor could not hope to overtake him on his wavering legs.

But a bullet has speed.

The roar was appalling. Victor tasted the nausea of absolute fear as Mack faltered, took a step, then sank slowly to the floor across the threshold to the studio. Victor's terror was so profound that the slightest sound would have led him to turn his gun against his own temple.

But the seconds passed, there was no outcry, no alarm, no hue and cry. At last, a single word scratched at his fogged mind: soundproofed. The impenetrable walls which confined Mack's melodies to the studio had also suppressed the gunshot. No one had heard.

The thought brought strength to his shaky legs and color to his ashy cheeks. He staggered from his crouch and went to the coat Mack had tossed on a chair. The wallet was bulging with greenbacks. Victor transferred the money to his pocket and threw aside the empty wallet. He felt in the coat pockets and found them stuffed haphazardly with wads of money. He caught glimpses of thousand-dollar bills among the more lowly hundreds. It looked as if Mack had cleaned the card, following his coup on the Daily Double.

Victor pulled the long-visored cap over his eyes, stepped over Mack's body and went to the penthouse door. He peered out. The central corridor was empty. He slipped out and gained the fire door. He was quite cool now; he even remembered that on his trip up, he had not worn Band-Aids and was careful to wipe off the doorknobs both on the penthouse floor and on his own floor. Again he looked through a crack in the fire door, saw that the corridor leading to his room was empty and darted to his door, his room key out and ready. In a second, he was inside, tearing off the cap and coveralls.

Jessie hurried to him, devouring him with her eyes, trying to gauge the situation without questions. She knew he hated to be catechized. He always told her everything but in his own good time. She never mentioned the agonies she suffered while he was on a job. She felt obscurely that the tougher she appeared, the more he approved of her. Now she schooled her voice to a breezy lightness. "Mission accomplished, I gather?"

He mumbled a reply as he stuffed the gun and the rest of the stuff into the zippered bag. His voice was not yet under control. It was just being borne in on him that he had killed a man—no; not just a man, but an outstanding figure in the contemporary scene, a man whose death would shock and inflame the whole nation, and whose murderer would be hunted and hounded by the best brains and the most relentless investigators in America.

Jessie stared at him worriedly. Something was wrong. There was none of the noisy effervescence that usually followed his successful strokes. She tried a timid question: "Vic, everything's all right, isn't it?"

He cleared his throat to gain time. He couldn't tell her now. He wanted her to walk out of the hotel with the debonair unconcern of an ordinary guest.

"Sure is, baby," he said with hollow heartiness. He went toward the bathroom and spoke over his shoulder: "Get on your hat and ring down for a bellboy. I'll be with you in a jiffy."

In the bathroom, as he began to remove the Band-Aids, his heart turned over: the Band-Aid on his left thumb was missing. His eyes started from his head and his face turned a sick green. Of all times in the world for this to happen! He began to curse Lee Mack under his breath because he knew exactly how it must have happened. When Mack had hit him, he had saved himself from going down altogether by snatching at a chair. And he remembered now a sharpness, a pointed carved artifice: the chair's arms had been contrived grotesquely to end in carved hands, each finger spread, complete with macabre sculptured fingernails. He had noticed it before Mack had arrived and now it came back to plague and destroy him. For one dizzy second, he had thoughts of retracing his path to the penthouse to retrieve the telltale Band-Aid but his legs turned to water from pure fear. He simply could not do it.

He tore off the remaining Band-Aids, stuffed them in his pocket to get rid of later, washed his hands and dashed cold water over his gray face. He rubbed a trace of color into his cheeks with a towel and came back into the bedroom, necessity winning a close battle over panic. The new situation required new strategy.

"Now, get this," he told Jessie. "I don't bring the

car to the door. When we get downstairs, we take a taxi. I tell him Grand Central. When we get there, I let him, get out of sight. Then I take another taxi back to the street where the car's parked. I stall until he drives off, then I put our stuff in the car and we're on our way. That clear?"

"Yes, Vic. But why— Did anything—?"

"Later. Phone down for a boy."

The last thing he did before the boy arrived was to wipe off the furniture, light switches, window sills and bathroom fixtures to remove all fingerprints.

Three-quarters of an hour later they were heading for the West Side Highway at a sedate pace, a personable young couple in a conservative black Buick, out for a holiday drive.

There was little talk between them. Jessie was diffident about forcing the conversation and Victor was thinking with all his powers of concentration. He considered: "What have they got? One Band-Aid for sure. Maybe they'll think Mack dropped it himself and think nothing of it. No. That's out. The damned foundation cream. They'll know the murderer had it on. So what? I'm not the only operator who uses Band-Aids instead of gloves. It won't bring them any closer to me. The real rub is, did I leave any fingerprints? Let's see. Left thumb. On the chair arm? I doubt it. I had the Band-Aid on when I grabbed it. So no prints. When I pulled myself up is when it tore loose. I didn't touch the chair arm again, so that's okay. What else? Oh—oh. The wallet. That does it. I sure as hell handled the wallet with both hands. One thumb print. What does that get them? I've never been booked so they've got no set of my prints in the record. We were registered as Mr. and Mrs. Thomas Benson of North Attleboro, Mass., and the bellboy heard me tell the taxi driver Grand Central. So how far can a lone thumb print take 'em toward William Chase of Crawfey? Not a step.

"Wait a minute. There's one snag. Murder by a man wearing Band-Aids. They'll link that up with Grotz in California—also a murder by a man wearing Band-Aids. What do they call it?—modus operandi. Well, Grotz is dead so he can't finger me. All they've got is a description from him and the Carver guy. Brown hair. Blue eyes. Heavy eyebrows. About thirty. Five-eleven. A hundred and seventy pounds. As Jimmy Durante used to say, 'There's a million of 'em.' All I've got to do is sit still. No more jobs, though, for a good long time. The guy who chilled Lee Mack's going to be plenty hot for months. Well, that's no problem. I'll have time to set out a real truck farm in Crawfey and pay some attention to Hewitt's Hardware. I'll have to think up a real good excuse to the natives for quitting the paper-box job. Because, brother, I'm sticking to Crawfey, as of now, till the heat's off.

"What about Jessie? How's she going to take this? I can't keep it from her because even a hole-in-the-ground like Crawfey's bound to hear about a guy as prominent as Mack. She's smart. As soon as the radio spills about the Hotel Cleveland and the money Mack won at the track, she'll remember the Daily Double guy and know why we left the track and who did the job. How will it hit her? How much have I got on her? She's in the burglary racket with me up to her neck. But murder? Will she hold still for that? Sure she will, the way she feels about me. She'd just about walk through fire if I said to. So that's okay.

"I wonder what the haul is. From the way my pockets are bulging, it looks like important money."

It was. When he counted it at Hewitt's Farm, it came close to twenty-nine thousand dollars. He did it upstairs in the bedroom while Jessie was preparing a scratch meal of canned goods, since all the shops were closed on account of the holiday. As he stacked the money in neat piles, he snickered ghoulishly, "It sure was Mack's lucky day."

As they ate tinned ham, baked beans and frozen strawberries along with Jessie's clear strong coffee, a sense of well-being pervaded Victor. Crawfey seemed a cozy paradise, a snug port in a storm. The odd thing was that he began to welcome his forced sojourn there. He looked forward to the simple local activities with pleasure. He was essentially a man who would prefer to be a big frog in a small pond. And Crawfey was small indeed. He would make himself felt in a dozen ways: how about donating a bandstand for the park and organizing a teen-age band to play there Saturday nights? The kids would go for it at his suggestion; they liked him. A warming thought. He mentioned it to Jessie and as usual she vetoed anything that would make him conspicuous.

"Darling, it's out of line. Even a regional manager for a big company doesn't make that kind of money."

"The paper-box job is out—as of now."

She set down her coffee cup.

"Vic, what do you mean?"

"I'm going Crawfey, one hundred per cent."

"But—what excuse will we have when we go away on . . . jobs?"

"We won't be going for a good while to come."

She stared at him for a full minute.

"Vic, something did happen today."

He came around the table to her, half lifted her out of her chair and murmured, "Forget that, honey. Come on."

Her housewifely soul made an automatic protest: "But the dishes, darling—"

"Hell with the dishes, baby. Must I carry you up?"

Five minutes later, as he held her close in the dark, he said, "You were right, honey. Something did happen today."

"Tell me later," she whispered, clinging to him.

"No. Now. I owe it to you."

"Owe it—? Vic—" The dread in her voice told him she half guessed. That was a help.

"Jessie, baby, a hell of a thing happened. The fool guy went haywire. He grabbed for the gun—we struggled—it went off—"

"Is he . . . ?"

"I don't know. I got out of there fast."

Her tense body strained away from him in shock—even in abhorrence, he thought, and he knew he had to act fast. He loosened his arms and said diffidently:

"I'm a louse, honey, to mix you up in this. I see that now. Well, thank God, there's still time to put it right."

"What do you mean?"

"Baby, I'm hot as a three-dollar pistol, so I'm getting out of here. If they catch me, I'll give a false name and keep you out of it."

The tenseness in her was still there but the abhorrence was all gone as she clutched him around the neck.

"Vic, no! You can't leave me! You're all I've got—"

"That goes double, baby." He bent his head, his lips seeking hers. "You think it's easy to give you up?"

"Don't go, darling," she said, straining closer. "I can't let you go. They won't find you here—and we'll be together."

His last drowsy self-satisfied thought before he slept was right in character, "Frankie Edwards—Victor Clyde —William Chase—it just takes brains."

CHAPTER FOURTEEN

At seven-fifteen the same evening Donald Tanner came into the Hotel Cleveland and stopped at the desk. Being the other half of the famous Mack-Tanner team, the "words" of "words and music by . . ." he was well known to the management and was greeted cordially. He said: "Will you give Mack a ring and say I'm waiting?"

"Certainly, Mr. Tanner." The desk clerk lifted his phone, got the switchboard and put in the call. After a pause, he said, "No answer. He doesn't seem to be in, sir."

"Sure he's in. I dropped him off an hour ago."

"I'll have the girl ring again."

But a series of rings produced no results. Tanner's smiling face smiled no longer.

"That's damn funny. He knows I'm picking him up."

"Probably he's in the shower and doesn't hear."

"He'd be in and out of the shower long ago. Keep ringing, will you."

At seven-thirty Tanner, now really puzzled, said, "I'd better go up. He might have slipped in the shower at that."

"I'll have the bell-captain go up with you to let you in, just in case, Mr. Tanner."

A few minutes later, Tanner and the middle-aged bell-captain, Duffy, stepped out of the elevator on the penthouse level. Duffy rang Mack's bell and after a few moments' wait with no result, used his master key.

The prone body, lying across the threshold between the studio and the bedroom was instantly visible. Tanner rushed forward, shouting, "Lee! What's the matter?" and bent over him.

He froze with horror at what he saw. Duffy came close, looked, crossed himself and gasped, "He—he's gone, God rest him, sir. All that blood—I'd best get the manager." He reached for the studio phone.

Howard Staden, capable, suave, distinguished, as befitted the manager of the dignified Hotel Cleveland, was located in his own apartment and was on the spot in three minutes. Some of his air of a major ambassador left him when he saw Mack. His healthy color faded and his usually firm voice shook as he said with something like anguish, "It's a police matter."

Police in the Cleveland. Staden shuddered but he knew his duty. He was knowledgeable in other ways too. Meg Wiley—Meg Hatfield, she was then—had gone to Sarah Lawrence with Staden's daughter and the two were still close friends. He himself had met the Wileys socially a few times and he felt if the sacred portals of the Cleveland had to be darkened by police, there was no one as acceptable as Lieutenant Lance Wiley of Homicide. He called Homicide East.

He was lucky in finding Lance on duty at nearly 8 p.m. on a holiday. He was winding up a peculiarly troublesome case of child murder and had decided to wait until his man was actually in custody before calling it a day. Another half hour would see him on his way home to Riverdale and a latish dinner. Staden's call changed all that.

Lance gave terse orders to alert the local precinct nearest the Cleveland, the D.A.'s office, the Medical Examiner and the technical men. Then he and Sergeant Knight were speeding up the Avenue, the siren cutting the soft near-summer air.

Ten minutes later, in the penthouse, after a long look at the dead man, Lance was given the meager details of the discovery of Lee Mack's body. He turned to the manager, "I want to talk to the elevator man who took Mack up. Find him and send him up, please." Then turning to Donald Tanner, he said incisively: "Now then, let's have it all."

"All? What—?"

"Begin at the beginning."

"You mean today? All we did?"

"That's what I mean."

"Well, we had a date to go to the races. We used my car, got to Belmont about 12:30 and had a bite in the Clubhouse."

"Meet anyone you knew?"

"Plenty of acquaintances. Nobody special."

"Did you stay to the end?"

"Yes. I wanted to leave after the seventh to beat the traffic but Lee was having a terrific run of luck. I couldn't get him away."

"Was he a big bettor?"

"Depends what you call big."

"Give me an idea."

"Well, he had a hundred on the Double. And he won it. That netted him about ten grand. Ordinarily, he'd bet one or two hundred to a race but today he began to plunge—five hundred and even a thousand. He kept saying: 'It's their money.' And it was uncanny. He couldn't seem to go wrong. He came home loaded."

"How much would you say he won?"

"More than twenty thousand, I guess. I wouldn't know exactly."

"Wouldn't you, Mr. Tanner?"

Don Tanner's eyes opened wide.

"Say—" he began angrily. Then he pulled himself together and spoke softly but with intense feeling, "Look, mister. I—loved the guy. I'm frozen now but losing Lee's like amputating an arm. I know you can't bring him back, but for God's sake find the bloody murderer who did him in and don't waste time suspecting me."

"I didn't say I suspected you, Mr. Tanner," Lance said noncommittally. "Go on with your story. What time did you reach New York after the races?"

"After six. Maybe twenty after. I dropped him at the entrance and went on home."

"Where's that?"

Tanner gave an address on East Sixty-third Street.

"Wait a minute," he said. "I took my car to the garage first, then walked the block to my house."

"And were back here again in an hour. Why?"

"We were going to have dinner and then do some work on a song."

"Why split up at all? Why didn't you come right up here at 6:20 with him?"

"On account of my mother. She's an invalid and we have kind of a habit to—to visit together before I go out for the evening. It makes her feel good. . . . I guess I like it, too."

"Go on."

"Well, I spent about fifteen minutes with her, then I took a shower and walked back over here. It's only three blocks. You know the rest."

"To your knowledge, did Mack have any enemies?"

"Absolutely not. Lee was a guy that everybody loved."

He broke off before his voice got out of control. "What about women?"

"Nobody special. Nobody who would—"

Staden came in with a white-faced elevator boy. "This is the boy who took Mr. Mack up, Lieutenant," he said.

Lance turned to the boy.

"Remember the time?" he asked.

"Not exactly. Six—six-thirty—"

"You don't remember the time but you do remember Mr. Mack?"

"Yes, sir. I only begin to watch the time around eight when I go off," he said naïvely. "But I sure do remember Mr. Mack. He—he's always free with tips but tonight he gave me five bucks! Why wouldn't I remember?"

"Was the elevator full?"

"So-so. Maybe four or five. I can't say exactly."

"Anyone but Mr. Mack for this floor?"

"No, sir, that's for sure, because after the rest got out and we were alone, I really thanked him."

"Anyone in the outside hall when you let him off?"

"Not a soul."

"Sure of that?"

"Well, look for yourself. There's no place a person could hide. And I saw Mr. Mack go into his apartment with my own eyes. We always wait till a penthouse guest gets in. That's a rule."

The enormous studio began to fill—precinct men, detectives from the district, an assistant Medical Examiner, and the photography and fingerprint men. The place became as busy as an assembly line. The precinct captain and the district detective-lieutenant conferred with Lance while the M.E. turned his attention to the body of Lee Mack.

From the moment Lance had entered the penthouse, Sergeant Knight had been unobtrusively busy. A round-cheeked boyish-looking man, he was deceptively guileless looking. But his mild eyes were sharp; not an inch of the roomy apartment escaped his notice.

The precinct captain took over the questioning of Staden, all the elevator boys who had been on duty that day and the Hotel Cleveland security officer, Farley, a bulldog ex-detective, aggressively sure that no criminal could have slipped into the sacred zone of the hotel without his spotting him. Lance had a moment's breathing space and caught Sergeant Knight's speaking eye. The two men retired to the comparative privacy of the bathroom and Knight reported:

"Couple of things, Lance. A wallet—his, I judge. It

was tossed on the floor, empty. I gave it to the print boys, although," he added with disgust, "is there a living soul who don't know about prints nowadays? As soon as they're finished with it, you better smell it."

"Smell it?"

"Yes, sir. See if you get what I got. If you do, the only other find I made might be something."

"What's that?"

"This. Found it in the bedroom under a funny-looking chair." He held out a cellophane envelope containing a single Band-Aid. "I wouldn't have given it much thought except it's smeared all over with some kind of tan-colored stuff."

Lance sniffed at it and then said, "The wallet smells the same. That what you mean?"

"That's right. I figure the killer used Band-Aids instead of gloves, colored flesh color to blend with his skin. Something new every day," he grinned.

Lance frowned in concentration.

"This isn't new," he said slowly. "I seem to remember . . . wait—I've got it— There was a killing on the Coast a few months ago— Dave, call Centre Street right away, ask 'em to get it on the teletype—"

"Frisco or L.A.?"

"L.A., I'm pretty sure. But try both. I want all the details they've got."

"Will do." He went to the phone and Lance made his way into the big modern kitchen where the fingerprint man was at work.

"Any luck with the wallet, Ellis?" he asked.

"You bet, Lieutenant. One perfect thumb print. And a lot of greasy smears. I've got my pictures so you can handle it."

Lance held the wallet to his nose to Ellis's amusement. "I noticed that too. Smells like a beauty parlor. What was the killer—a nance?"

"I doubt it. He wore Band-Aids and for some

reason tinted them with a colored cream.”

“Hey! Band-Aids! Remember, Lieutenant, a couple of weeks ago that heist case—?”

“Homicide doesn’t hear much about anything but murder. What about it?”

“I don’t recall the name but it was at the Rogers on Forty-eighth Street. The guy who was held up said the burglar wore tape on his fingers but they called me anyway on, the chance I might get some incomplete fingertip prints. I didn’t but I sure got a load of that smell on his wallet.”

“That’s a help, Ellis. Gives us a starting point.”

Lance called the precinct covering West Forty-eighth Street and asked for details about any robbery at the Rogers in the past few weeks. The desk sergeant had facts and names at his fingertips, having been on duty at the time. Lance asked him to send a man to the Rogers to pick up Pinelli and bring him to Homicide East for questioning. Then he went back to the studio and sought out the house-detective, Farley.

“What’s the ground floor exit to those fire stairs?”

“They open into the package room behind the lounge.”

“Is there an outside exit from the package room?”

“Yes. To the delivery entrance. You got something to deliver, you leave it there. We deliver it to the guests.”

“There’s someone on duty at all times?”

“Round the clock. We’ve had medicine sent in at 4 a.m.”

“And no one could get past the package clerk and deliver something personally?”

“Not a stick of celery.” The house-detective’s bulldog jaw jutted defensively. “What’s more, today being a holiday, the delivery entrance gates were closed and locked besides. Anybody with anything to deliver today had to ring the outside bell on the gate even to get to the package-room door. First thing I did when Mr. Staden told me about this mess was check our man on duty down there. He says it was quiet as a church all day. Only two deliveries—in the morning—both boxes of flowers. Take it from me, Lieutenant, nobody got in or up through there."

"We've talked to every elevator boy on duty. The only person taken up to this floor all day long was Mack himself around 6:20. The tenants of the other three penthouses are away over the week-end. And you say nobody got up through the fire stairs. You see where that leaves us? Either an employee or a guest."

Farley looked as if Lance had assailed his mother's good name. He began to bluster but Lance cut him short. "I want you to co-operate with Sergeant Knight on every guest in the hotel—"

"You can't do this—we can't insult— This is the *Cleveland*—!"

"That's up to you, Farley. Use your head and your tact. Find out where every guest was from six to seven-thirty. Put it that you're questioning to find out if they saw something suspicious. Everybody loves to have a finger in a murder pie."

"Not our guests."

"You'd be surprised how human nature is alike whether it's the Cleveland or a fleabag. Also I want you to check in detail on every employee."

"Lieutenant, we employ hundreds!"

"Then you've got a full night's work," Lance said coolly. "Nobody goes off duty till he's been screened. That clear?"

Farley gave a sullen nod and went out with Knight and two district detectives who were delegated to assist in the colossal job.

The body of Lee Mack had been removed to the morgue to await autopsy. The police photographer had finished his work, the precinct men had the routine business well in hand. There was little Lance could do on the spot. He decided he could be more useful in his own office. Before he left, he stepped once more into the kitchen to speak to the print man.

"Rush that thumb print to C.B.I., Ellis. If it's on file—"

"I got its brother, Lieutenant. Off a chair—if you can call it that."

"What do you mean?"

"Come in the bedroom and look. It's the cock-eyedest piece of furniture I ever saw."

In the bedroom Ellis pointed out the chair whose arms ended in a carved representation of outspread fingers.

"Can you beat that? What'll they dream up next?"

"Show me just where you found it."

"Here, on the outside of the hand, near the wrist."

"On the right arm!"

"Yeah," said Ellis, struck. "Now how would his left hand get on the right arm?"

"Not while he was sitting in it, that's sure." Lance stared down at the chair. Then he stooped and sniffed the wooden fingers. "Same smell. That sharp pinky fingernail could account for the killer losing the Band-Aid. Knight said he found it under a funny-looking chair. If the killer caught it on the point of the nail, it could rip off easy."

"Sure could. You could rip skin off on that thing if you weren't careful."

"But he would have noticed it was gone." Lance's eyes narrowed in thought. "And if he noticed, he never would have touched the wallet with his bare thumb. So we can take it he didn't notice. Now how can a man lose a thing like that without noticing?"

"You tell me, Loot." Ellis grinned.

"It took a pretty violent move to rip it off. The only way it could miss attention would be if something much more violent was going on."

"You mean, Mack and the killer tangled? Yeah—"

"And the killer was getting the worst of it. He grabbed at the chair, the Band-Aid tore off—Mack got past him and was nearly out into the studio when the killer stopped him with a bullet."

"Sounds fine, Lieutenant, but where does it get you?"

"Not far." Lance smiled. "Except in the 'modus operandi' department. It tells us a little bit about the killer."

"It don't tell me a thing."

"Well, he isn't essentially a killer or he'd have used the gun before Mack moved. Just kills if he's in a tight corner. So he could easily be your heist-artist from the Rogers. If Mack hadn't resisted, he'd probably still be alive."

"Poor devil. He was a great guy. I always listened to him on TV."

"You and about fifty million others."

"Yeah, this is gonna raise a hell of a stink."

"Too right. The top brass will be breathing down our necks till we land the killer."

"You'll land him, Lieutenant. They don't call you Wily Wiley for nothing."

"I've been lucky." Lance shrugged and grinned.

"I should have that kind of luck. I wouldn't be shooting powder and dusting if off like a doggone housemaid."

Back at Homicide East, Lance found a sullen but wary Pinelli waiting for him.

"What gives? Arresting a man when he's clean as a whistle?" he complained.

"Arresting? You're all wrong, Mr. Pinelli. We simply sent for you to ask your help," Lance said blandly.

"Help? I know from nothing. What kind of a stall is this?"

"Now. Now. Let me explain. There's been another holdup like the one you suffered a couple of weeks ago. We think it's the same man. So we'd like a few more details about him from you."

"I told the cop all I knew at the time."

"That's right. You were most co-operative, I understand, but I didn't get the details from you as it wasn't my case. So I'd like you to repeat it all for me."

Pinelli's black eyes narrowed shrewdly.

"This is Homicide East. Somebody get croaked?"

"Yes, I'm afraid so."

"Well, I don't want any part of it. Get your details from the cop I talked to."

Lance's pleasant blue eyes were suddenly as cold as Arctic ice. He recognized Pinelli's type, even though he knew nothing incriminating about him at the moment. He took a chance. He spoke to the patrolman at the door.

"Egan, hold this man as a material witness."

"Now wait a minute—" Pinelli howled.

"Take him away."

"You can't do this—I'm clean—I got an alibi as tight as a drum—"

The patrolman stepped forward slowly, giving Pinelli time to cave in.

Lance said softly: "Alibi? For what time, Mr. Pinelli? And a clean man doesn't obstruct justice."

"I ain't ob— All right, all right. I'll talk, if it's so important. I come home about six that night, go up to my room and here's this goon in a Hallowe'en mask pointin' a .38 at me. I go for my—I mean I open my mouth to yell and he conks me with the gaf. That's all of it."

"Not quite. What about his fingers?"

"Yeah. He don't wear gloves. He's got tape on all his fingers."

"White?"

"Sure—" Pinelli frowned. "Uh—no—light tan—"

"You see, Mr. Pinelli," said Lance, now cordial

again. "Right at the start you've helped us find a new fact."

Pinelli shot him a sour look.

"So it was tan. What does that get you?"

"It confirms our belief that the same man did both jobs."

"Well, go find him. I'd like my seven—" He shut up fast.

"I don't blame you," Lance said smoothly. "Seven thousand dollars is a lot of money."

"I never said seven thousand," said Pinelli quickly.

"No, but we have reason to believe it was."

Pinelli's doughy face was suddenly suffused with dark blood.

"Say—if I'm bein' tailed—"

"Tailed, Mr. Pinelli? Now why should you think that?"

"That's the only way you could know what I won—" Again he broke off short.

Lance sat very still. Lee Mack, after a phenomenal day at the races, was robbed and murdered. Pinelli, after winning seven thousand dollars somewhere, was attacked and robbed.

Lance said very casually: "Do you go on information or do you handicap the horses yourself?"

"Who said anything about horses?" Pinelli muttered.

Lance thought fast and went on with his bluff:

"Mr. Pinelli, I'm a Homicide man. I'm not interested in whether you've been barred from the New York tracks or why. But if you withhold information in a murder case, you'll find yourself in bad trouble."

"Okay, so I won some money at Jamaica," he said sullenly. "The crook who robbed me didn't know that. He was there in my room ahead of me."

"Do you often go to the track?"

"Now and then."

"How often?"

"Pretty regular." Then he added insolently: "I believe in the improvement of the thoroughbred."

"I'm sure you do," Lance said unruffled. "Now I want as good a description of the holdup man as you can give me."

"Look. I had about a split second before he beaned me. I can't tell you a thing."

"How tall was he?"

"Taller than me—maybe five eleven—six feet—"

"Voice?"

"What can you tell from behind a mask? He says 'This is a stickup' and wham, I'm out."

"Foreign accent?"

"No. Strictly American."

"Notice his clothes?"

"Yeah—I did—he had on coveralls. It comes back to me."

"Anything else?"

"Not a thing."

"Well, thanks, Mr. Pinelli. You may go." Pinelli shot out of the office with more speed than seemed possible for his flabby physique. Lance sat at his desk in sharp thought.

Two men, lucky at the track, robbed in their own homes by a man who was already there when they arrived. Coincidence? He didn't think so. Both times, the robber wore Band-Aids tinted flesh-color with cream. Had Lee Mack's assailant worn a Hallowe'en mask as Pinelli's had? Lance believed he had.

Egan came back after seeing Pinelli off the premises. "Lieutenant, there's a raft of newspaper men yammering for a statement."

Lance sighed. It was beginning. Lee Mack's murder was going to raise a furor bigger than anything since the Lindbergh case. He glanced at his wrist watch. He pulled his phone toward him and asked the board for his home number. It was his habit to call Meg at eleven when he was working overtime.

"Meg, honey? Trouble. Expect me when you see me."

CHAPTER FIFTEEN

At 7:30 a.m. after a three-hour sleep on a cot at Homicide East, Lance was back at his desk. It was piled high with reports. Detectives had dug deep into Lee Mack's daily life, had interviewed his agent, his manager, his music publisher, the recording people and the TV studio to whom he was under contract. There was not a single lead. It was as Don Tanner had stated. Mack was as lovable and loved a man in private as he was in public. The only reaction the detectives elicited was shock and sorrow. And Lance accepted this as genuine. He firmly believed Mack's death was a felony murder, committed during the course of a simple holdup.

He was still reading when Sergeant Knight, red-eyed and unshaven, walked in, a sheaf of scribbled notes in his hand.

"That was quite a job," he said with a watery grin. "Just finished and it'll take me all day to get out even a UF61 report. So I thought I better come and give you the highlights."

"Good. Sit down before you fall down, Dave."

Knight dropped into a chair and Lance held out a pack of cigarettes. When they both had lighted up, Knight said, "How do you tape it, Lance?"

"Just what it looks like. Murder during the commission of a burglary."

"You don't think the empty wallet could be a blind to hide a private grudge-killing? He didn't touch Mack's jewelry or those little gold statues on the mantel."

"This bird is interested strictly in hard cash."

Knight gave him a sharp glance.

"Hey, you're way ahead of me. What have you got?"

"A man named Pinelli was held up in his hotel room recently and robbed of seven thousand dollars he had won that day at the races. When he resisted, the burglar conked him with his gun. Lee Mack makes a terrific winning at Belmont, comes home and is held up the moment he gets in. I believe he resisted, too. And so effectively that a rap with the gun wasn't enough. So he was shot."

Egan came in with some papers in his hand.

"For you, Chief. Just came in on the teletype." Egan went out and Lance devoured the long message absorbedly. At last he looked up:

"This is from L.A., Dave, in answer to our request. On March 7th, Herman Grotz comes home to his hotel from the races, is held up by a man in a Hallowe'en mask, already in his room, and when he resists, is conked with the butt of a gun. But not until after he pulls off the robber's mask and gets a look. He recovers and gives the police a good description. Twenty-four hours later, Grotz drops dead from the delayed effects of a depressed skull fracture. L.A.'s got a Murder One on its hands. They looked into recent holdups and discover another with the same modus op., except that the victim, a man named Carver, co-operates and is uninjured."

Knight groaned.

"One of these lone wolf characters. One needle in a hundred and sixty million haystacks!"

"Wait. There's more. In both cases, some nosy neighbors noticed a car standing for hours near the victims' homes. And what a car! The iris Cadillac. Remember it, a couple of years ago? A lovely lavender color. You didn't look at it twice. You looked three or four times."

"Did they trace it?" Knight's eyes snapped with

interest.

"Don't be funny. In Hollywood? Anywhere else in America a car like that'd stick out like a sore thumb. So far the L.A. police have run down a hundred and seventy-six iris Cadillacs locally and they're still finding 'em."

"It's our baby now," Knight said gloomily. "That Caddy's sure as hell in New York along with its owner. You want me to get on to it?"

"We'll have to, I suppose. But it's my guess he ditched it long ago."

"Too hot?"

"Sure. The guy reads the papers. Show me a crook who doesn't when there's news about himself."

"Well, the odds are going down," said Knight sardonically. "Now it's one needle in only eight million haystacks."

"Much less than that, Dave. I believe Farley, the Cleveland house-dick, and the elevator boys. I don't think any stranger got up to the penthouse floor through the stairs or elevators."

"Making it an inside job."

"Right. That's why you lost your beauty sleep." Lance grinned. "I wanted a microscope on every employee and guest who was on the premises yesterday. It looks like the killer has to be among them.

"Yeah but—" Knight began dubiously. "I've got notes on 'em all. We did the guests from 8 to 1 a.m. The manager Staden went around with me, Farley went with one of the district detectives and the assistant manager with the other one. There were only three hundred and nine guests in the hotel during the critical time. We got a break there on account of the holiday. A lot of 'em were away. Same with the help. There was only a skeleton crew on, you might say—two hundred and twelve of 'em. Usually—Lance, you won't believe me—but Staden tells me that the Cleveland averages three employees to every guest!"

"I do," said Lance dryly. "I understand the ratio determines the standing of a hotel. Three to one, first-class. Two to one, second class and so on down to the fleabags. Well, go on with your story."

"We tackled them after we finished with the guests. That took us longer."

"Why?"

"Well, with the guests we couldn't do any real grilling. Staden, Farley and the assistant manager saw to that. In my case, the routine went something like this: Staden would say, 'Good evening, Mr. Astorbilt, so sorry to trouble you, but we need your help. Did you, by any chance (chahnce, I mean) observe any strange person about, from ha-alf pa-ast five until ha-alf pa-ast seven?' The best I could do was keep my eyes open and take a few notes about each guest. It worked out the same way for the others. Their reports show it. But I'll say this: there didn't seem to be a phony in the whole lot. They all looked to be honest-to-God solid citizens, mostly over sixty years old, plenty of 'em well known. Young ones evidently haven't got the dough it takes to breathe Cleveland air. The few kids there were looked to be honeymooners—damn the expense once in a lifetime."

"And the help?"

"Well, it'd have to be a conspiracy with about twenty members if the killer was among them."

"How's that?"

"The Cleveland's got an organizational system that General Motors couldn't better. From the top down, there's somebody in charge at every level. Bellboys, waiters, chambermaids, kitchen help—if anybody so much as goes to the john, his immediate superior knows it. And checks how long he's gone. Practically every minute of a worker's time is superintended and accounted for."

"Bunk! A bellboy could get a room call, attend to it in five minutes, spend fifteen more doing the Mack job and come down and report the call took twenty minutes."

"Not today with only a skeleton crew on. And that was one point where the guest job helped. Staden did check with everybody as to whether they had sent for a 'page boy'—not bellhop, nothing so common— or a room-waiter or even a chambermaid, so that later we were able to check the guest's report against the help's report. Not a single discrepancy in point of time. What's more, from six—before Mack got home—until seven, fifty per cent of the help were eating their dinner in the Employees' Cafeteria and strictly clean. They eat in shifts. The other fifty per cent were on duty and were kept hopping. If one of 'em had been on a job five minutes longer than he should have been, he'd have been on the carpet and we'd know it."

"How about the chefs and kitchen help and dining-room waiters?"

"They alibi each other. That's why I say it'd have to be a mass job. Twenty men aren't going to lie to cover one, are they? And the quality of the help is something. Everyone is investigated up to the hilt before he rates to be employed by the holy Cleveland."

"So we write off the employees?"

"To my way of thinking."

"And you're pretty sure of the guests, too?"

"There could be a slick operator among them, I guess. But they looked good. Nothing you could put a finger on."

"You give the help and the guests a clean bill. Nobody slipped in from the outside—"

"Wait a minute, Lance. How's this? A guy—well-dressed, of course—goes up in the elevator. Asks for the twentieth floor, say, gets out and walks up the fire stairs to the penthouse floor—"

"No dice. Didn't you notice there's a floor-clerk sitting at a desk on every floor outside the elevators?"

"Sure, but the fire door's around a corner out of sight of the floor-clerk."

"The Cleveland thought of that too, Dave. They really do protect their guests."

"You tell me."

"A stranger gets out of the elevator on your twentieth floor, say. The floor-clerk stops him, asks who he wants and who he is, then punches a switchboard and announces him to the guest he's trying to visit. If the guest okays him, he gets the nod. Otherwise, nix. The whole procedure's polite as hell but nobody unaccounted for gets by the floor-clerk."

"Well then, where the hell was the penthouse floor-clerk at the crucial time?"

"That's the weak link. There isn't one. There are only four tenants on that floor. Hardly warrants paying for a day and night floor-clerk. The Cleveland may be holy but they're not above saving a fast buck. Instead of a floor-clerk, they have a rule that the elevator boy who takes the penthouse tenant up stays and watches till he's safe in his apartment. That answer you?"

"Yeah, I guess. I'd vote for the elevator boy who took Mack up but he's out. He was down on the lobby floor within seconds—right on schedule. So where do we look next?"

Lance sat back and closed his eyes. Knight waited; he knew that trancelike stillness of Lance Wiley's well; he knew that behind the calm there was usually effective activity going on. Then the eyelids flew up and Lance leaned forward.

"Dave, you're a holdup man—de luxe, of course. Strictly for folding money. No jewelry, no Old Masters, no objects of art. In other words, no fence.

As you said, a lone wolf. You check in and live at the Cleveland. You pick a rich victim—"

"Now wait a minute. It costs heavy gold to live at the Cleveland. How does he know his haul will be worth it? Rich men pay by check, they don't carry much dough."

"I said he picked a victim. I didn't say where."

"Come again?"

"He picks him at the racetrack—Mack, Pinelli, Grotz—"

"Oh-oh. I get it. He stakes him out. Follows him until he makes a clean-up—trails him home—"

"No. He beats him home. Every time he's already inside when the victim comes in. He's evidently an artist on locks. Once inside, he puts on his mask and his Band-Aids and waits. When the victim walks in, he shoves a gun at him, ties and gags him, takes his winnings and leaves."

"Leaves? But the house-dick says nobody—"

"I said he left the victim's apartment. Not the hotel."

Knight groaned again.

"Lance, we'll have a riot if we really work over the guests. Some of 'em are big shots. They'll yammer to the top brass—"

"Before we do any grilling, I see one more possibility."

"I'm listening."

"As I said, you're a holdup man, living in the hotel. You make your haul. But your man—Mack— acts up and you have to kill him. You run out, get back fast to your own room. In your possession is a bankroll of some twenty thousand dollars, a gun, a mask, a box of Band-Aids and maybe a pair of coveralls—Pinelli said he wore 'em—and it's only a question of hours before the hotel will be swarming with cops who may or may not search the whole place. What would you do?"

"I'd get out as fast as—" Knight's eyes snapped. "I get it. Hey, boy, we've got it down to a needle in only ten or twenty haystacks. I'll go right up to the Cleveland and find out who checked out last night."

"I'll go myself. You'll go home and hit the hay for a few hours. Hear?"

CHAPTER SIXTEEN

The morning after their demure flight from the Cleveland, Vic watched Jessie covertly for signs of a sudden revulsion of feeling. He felt unpleasantly vulnerable at being at the mercy of any human being, especially one so unpredictable as Jessie. All the time he had known her, she had continually surprised him with her contrariness. At times when he had expected shocked disapproval, she had laughed. At others, she had enlarged a molehill of squeamishness into a mountain of scruples—as witness the day she had refused up and down to do the preliminary "casing" by phone because the victim was lame. Even after last night's complete capitulation, he was far from sure of her attitude in the cold light of morning.

A lucky trifle helped to swing things his way. He came back into the bedroom after shaving, his face fresh and vital-looking, his bare torso vigorous with dynamic energy. In his hand was an old stiff worn-out razor-strop. He said, "What's this thing cluttering up the bathroom for?"

To his surprise, Jessie turned white. She said harshly, "I don't know. Throw it away. Now. Right away, will you. I—hate it!" Then she flung herself at him, clinging desperately. "Vic. Vic. You're mine and I'm yours, no matter what!"

"Sure, baby," he said soothingly. "No matter what."

He remembered that the razor-strop had figured in

an ugly clash between Jessie and her father. If Crawfey represented a refuge to Vic, so did he represent one to Jessie.

It was therefore with assurance and an implication of firm partnership that he said at breakfast, "I'd better drive into New York and pick up the papers. May as well now what we're up against."

She accepted the plural pronoun and only said, "Shall go with you?"

"Better not. Your job is to lay down a smoke screen here. Go to market, drop the news that we're just back from—Birmingham, Alabama's a good spot—you might even get in a word that my 'firm' is merging with another and I don't like the new setup. Don't lug it in, understand. Just if it comes about naturally. Then I'll follow up the first time I play poker with the boys. The whole idea is to account for us staying here till this blows over."

"Vic, tell me just what happened."

"I did."

"You were never this worried before."

"My gun never went off before."

"You think he—he—"

"A .38 isn't a toy."

"But it might have just hit him in the arm or—"

"That's why I want to get the papers. So we know what we're up against."

"You don't have to drive all the way to New York. You can get them at any railway station along the line."

"I don't want any nosy Parkers in a little place remembering a stranger buying copies of every New York paper when the heat starts."

"Why buy them all? Any one of them will have the facts."

He straightened his shoulders and laughed. He spoke playfully but with an odd eagerness, "What say we start a scrapbook, baby? Might be fun."

She looked at him blankly.

"Anything you say," she agreed.

He drove Jessie's Dodge, leaving her the Buick to use for marketing. In spite of the fact that he had used only parking-lots for his car in New York and switched from one to another, he felt it was unwise to show himself and the Buick together while the hunt was on. He was supposed to be Thomas Benson of North Attleboro, Mass., who had left town last evening by train. If, inadvertently, a bellboy or a parking-lot attendant off duty caught a glimpse of him in New York when he should by rights be a couple of hundred miles away, it could raise questions in a smart boy's mind to the extent of his noting the Buick's license number. It was risky coming into town at all, but it was imperative in order to know just how far the police were getting in their investigation.

By the time he reached the metropolitan area, it occurred to him that the Dodge was equally dangerous. Its license could be traced to Crawfey as easily as the Buick's. He decided it was wise to buy his papers uptown and avoid midtown Manhattan. Accordingly, he parked on a side street near Broadway and walked to the subway kiosk at 168th Street. He pulled his hat far down over his eyes (Grotz's description in the Los Angeles papers had high-lighted Vic's arched eyebrows), collected his assortment of papers and threw some change on the stand. It was a slack hour and the man behind the counter had time for a comment, "New show open last night, mister?" he grinned.

Victor caught it instantly; grinned back and said, "That's right. Have to see if they panned me."

As he walked away with his packet of papers, he felt a rush of anger. Damned snooper. Well, tomorrow he'd avoid 168th Street like the plague. He'd come down the Concourse and try a Lexington Avenue newsstand. There was no question in his mind but that he would he coming down tomorrow. Wisdom demanded it. There was also a sharp exhilaration in the fact that the front-page news would be about him.

Before he went back to the car, he stopped at a drugstore and bought a bottle of peroxide. By tomorrow, the too noticeable eyebrows would be noticeable no longer.

He was itching to park somewhere on the way home and devour the news. But he curbed the desire. It might be conspicuous. He would wait. It was past noon when he arrived back at Hewitt's Farm. Jessie, with her unobtrusive efficiency, served lunch at once. She asked no questions, she made no move to appropriate one of the papers at his elbow. She kept her eyes on her plate. She, too, knew how to wait.

As Victor ate, he scanned the news for its high lights. Later, he would digest every column, sentence by sentence, but now he skimmed the cream only. There was not too much in the way of facts. The police had come on the case around 8 p.m., the reporters a little later, but not much had happened before the press deadlines. Lieutenant Lance Wiley (picture on Page 2) of Homicide East was in charge. A Band-Aid, tinted flesh color, had been found, presumably dropped by the murderer (Ellis, the fingerprint man had been clay in the hands of a persuasive reporter), linking the crime with a holdup some weeks previously at the Hotel Rogers with Mario Pinelli as victim. A solitary fingerprint on the wallet of the dead man was being rushed to Headquarters for identification. An early solution to the case seemed probable.

But where Mack himself was concerned, the papers spread themselves. Column after column, page after cage, was devoted to this beloved maker of his country's songs, to the joy he brought to the nation with his melodies, his personal charm and wit, his great charitable heart, his encouragement to beginners, his lavish expenditure of time and money to any and every worthy muse, his host of personal friends and the uncounted millions across the country who loved him.

America was in mourning.

Victor looked across the table at Jessie with a smile. "We sure picked on a top banana," he said lightly. "How'd you make out in the village?"

"I did what you said. Ada Hancock was at the grocer's and we talked."

"What did you say exactly? We want our stories to tally."

"I mentioned Birmingham and I said your firm was merging with another and you didn't like the new arrangement."

"Nice work. I can take it from there." He rose and stretched luxuriously. "You know—it's good to be home—I wonder if it's too late to lay out a flower garden for you."

"Vic—"

"Yeah, hon?"

"Did he—die?"

"Die?—Oh, Mack. Yes, he did. I told you a .38 was no joke. The damned fool. Why, the guy must be worth millions. So for a few lousy bucks, he fights like a tiger and gets shot in the scuffle."

"Do they—know anything?"

"The police? They do, at that. We had bad luck, baby. I lost a Band-Aid when Mack tangled with me. That'll show you how rough he played."

"But is that dangerous?"

"Well, I didn't notice it was gone and they've got my thumb print off his wallet."

She gave a strangled cry. He patted her shoulder and laughed.

"Calm yourself, kid. I'm not in the records. By the time they sort out that print from a hundred and sixty million people, I'll die of old age. Let's get the one o'clock news on the radio. Have to keep abreast of the times."

The one o'clock news contained much more meat. The autopsy revealed that Mack had been shot in the back. There were no powder burns, proof that the killer had not fired at close quarters. The police had ascertained that Mack's assailant was probably the same man wanted in Los Angeles for the murder of Herman Grotz, also killed in the course of a holdup. Progress in the California murder had been at a standstill but now, in view of the atrocious slaughter of Lee Mack, intensified efforts were being revived on the Coast. Renewed appeals to the public for information concerning the mauve Cadillac were being made. The Los Angeles Police were co-operating with New York to the fullest extent.

Vic snapped off the radio, his face red. He looked at Jessie and said harshly, "Okay. Now you know everything. Go ahead and turn me in."

She sat, paper-white, devouring him with her eyes.

"Is it true about this Grotz?" she asked.

"He pulled off my mask. I had to tap him so I could get clear away."

"But he—died."

"How was I to know he had a skull like a pecan? I tapped Pinelli, too, when he reached for his gun. But he didn't die. It was just bad luck with Grotz."

"Your gun didn't just go off in a scuffle with Lee Mack, did it? You shot him in the back from a distance."

"Here's how it was," he said defensively. "When he came in, I braced him with the gun and told him to reach. Instead, he slugged me. My chin's still sore. You can see the place. I fell and he started to run out to give the alarm. It was him or me. I had no thought of killing him. I tried to hit him low, just to stop him, just to give myself time to duck out. But I was shaken up by the sock he gave me and the shot went wild. Honest to God, honey, I'm no killer. It was just bad luck."

He stopped, eyeing her anxiously, feeling like a prisoner awaiting sentence. His whole life was in Jessie's hands. Her answer was a bombshell: "From now on, I'll go into town to buy the papers. It's much too dangerous for you to show your face in New York."

He let out his breath in a sharp hiss of relief. She went on talking, quietly, soberly, without inflection: "Listen, Vic. We can't go on like this. I hate all this violence. When you first told me about taking winnings away from bettors, it didn't sound so terrible—it was even funny—but—"

His face set in sullen lines.

"Okay, okay," he said angrily. "I can do without the sermon."

The tone frightened her; alerted all her senses to the weakness of her hold on him. She said hurriedly, "I don't want to make a speech—but—these killings—Vic—we don't need to go on with it— Hewitt's earns plenty for us to live on—"

"I'm not living on my wife's money, thanks."

"As if that mattered! Vic—don't you see— someday you won't get out of it—you'll be caught—"

"And the lily-white Hewitts'll be smeared," he gibed.

She came close and shook his arms.

"You know it isn't that. Vic, don't you know how I love you? I wouldn't want to live if anything happened to you."

He smiled at her in a lightning change of strategy. "You're a good kid, Jessie. I don't know what I ever did to deserve you."

"It's the other way round. Don't you realize you're the only person in the world who ever loved me and needed me?"

"I need you all right, baby."

"And you'll give up all this awful murder business?"

"Oh, sure," he promised glibly.

"I knew you would. It's not as if you were a bad person, darling. You're not a real killer—"

"It was just a lousy accident," he said, beginning to get restive.

"Of course. You don't have to tell me."

"I feel damn bad about it myself."

"I know. You couldn't do anything like that deliberately."

"Okay. We'll forget it. Forget it ever happened."

"We can't do that. We've got to follow things up—find out what they learn about it—protect ourselves—" She shivered. "If they caught you—if I lost you—!"

"No fear, baby. They'll never get close."

To end the awkward conversation, he picked up one of the papers. He turned to page 2 and for a long time stared at the pictured face of Lieutenant Lance Wiley of Homicide East. A slow derisive grin parted his lips.

CHAPTER SEVENTEEN

At 8:30 a.m. the same morning, Wiley, accompanied by Ellis, the fingerprint man, sat with Howard Staden in the latter's private office at the Cleveland. Staden was busy with a stack of registration cards. After a time, he gathered a small batch of them together, aligned their edges and looked up.

"Here you are, Lieutenant. May 30th. Twelve checkouts."

Lance took the cards and riffled through them quickly.

"We'll take them one by one, Mr. Staden. Give me all you've got on each of them."

In ten minutes, Lance had eliminated eight of them. The guests were either so well known as to be impossibilities or so old as to be improbabilities. He concentrated on the four remaining cards.

"Now, Mr. Staden, do you know these four ex-guests?"

"Let me think. H. L. Gross. Yes. We see him twice a year. Have for several years. Buyer for a New Orleans department store."

"Must be a cushy job to let him stop here."

"I believe he buys for several departments. Really a sales-manager."

"Would you describe him please?"

"About thirty-eight or forty. Less than average height—stocky—no, more than that. Obese would be the word. He must weigh close to two hundred."

"Face—features?"

"Well, the features are rather lost in the face. Tiny eyes, nose and mouth set in a moon face."

Lance tossed H. L. Gross onto the pile of discards and picked up another.

"Senor Ramon Alvarez and family. What about him?"

"An Argentinian. He was here with his wife and three little girls—"

"Does he speak good English?"

"None at all. We used an interpreter. One of our accountants."

Lance tossed the card on the pile of rejects, saying, "Pinelli says our man wasn't foreign-born." He picked up a third card. "Alexander Singer?"

"Mr. Singer is a stranger to us. He checked out to enter the Medical Center for orthopedic treatment. He walked with a decided limp."

"Could have been put on. We'll check with the Medical Center." He picked up the last card. "Mr.

and Mrs. Thomas Benson, 92 Pilhowie Avenue, North Attleboro, Mass. What about them? Will you describe them?"

"Benson—Benson—probably transients—I'm afraid I can't, Lieutenant."

"Who can?"

Staden scanned the particulars on the card.

"Checked in Monday, the 26th, 2 p.m. Hastings was on the desk. Shall I have him in?"

"Please."

Hastings remembered the Thomas Bensons with the phenomenal retentiveness of a good hotel man.

"Why, yes. A personable young couple. I put them down as honeymooners, very pleasant, very devoted, nothing—er—sinister about them—"

"They had reservations?"

"Yes. Made by phone."

"I'd like a physical description of them both."

"As I say, both of them were very attractive. The wife showed breeding—that special something you can spot at a glance. The man was a little cruder, very hearty and hail-fellow, but pleasing."

"His appearance?"

"A big fellow and well set up. Brown hair, a lot of it, good features. About the only thing distinctive about him was the eyebrows. Not shaggy, mind you, but they looked like they were stroked on with an eyebrow pencil." Lance held his breath. Hastings shrugged. "That's about all I can tell you."

"I notice his room is 2104," said Lance, glancing at the card. "Has that room been occupied since last night?"

"It will be by six o'clock. I made the reservation myself a little while ago."

"I'd like to go up there without delay." He nodded to Ellis who nodded back.

"Anything you say, Lieutenant," said the harassed Staden. "I'll go up with you."

The door to 2104 stood open. A pile of used linen was heaped on the floor and a chambermaid was attaching the plug of a vacuum cleaner to an outlet in the wall. Lance said, "Good morning. You're just starting to fix this room up?"

"Why, yes, sir. I only came on a little while ago."

"Fine." Lance breathed a sigh of relief. "Have you—ah—handled anything in here?"

"Just the bedding," the girl said, staring.

"Wonderful. Now, if you'll just go and do some other chores for a bit and leave the room to us—"

At a nod from Staden she left. The manager, too, went back to his duties. Lance closed the door and said to Ellis, "This is too good to be true. Pinpointing the man in a matter of minutes. How dumb can a crook get—walking around with eyebrows that stand out a mile?"

"I was just thinking, Loot. Plenty of men have bushy eyebrows. This guy Benson may be clean as a whistle."

"We'll soon see. I never did think much of coincidences. Get busy on every surface here and in the bathroom. Don't spare the powder." While Ellis set to work, Lance went to the phone and asked for long distance. "Give me Police Headquarters at North Attleboro, Massachusetts." When he had his connection, he identified himself and said, "Chief, I'm after some information about one of your citizens."

"Who would that be?" a drawling New England voice asked.

"Mr. Thomas Benson, of 92 Pilhowie Avenue."

"Come again with that address?"

"Ninety-two Pilhowie Avenue."

"We've got no such street here, sir."

"Perhaps some little road out in the country—?"

"No, sir. I've lived here fifty-nine years. I know North Attleboro, South Attleboro, Attleboro Falls and Attleboro itself like the back of my hand, and there's no Pilhowie Avenue in or near any of 'em."

"Well, is there a local Benson to your knowledge?"

"Yes, sir. Jared Benson. He's ninety-one years old and confined to a wheel-chair. That answer you?"

"Yes, Chief. I guess that really does answer me." He hung up slowly and said, "No coincidence, Ellis. Looks like Benson's our man."

"I'm thinking so too," said Ellis excitedly. "Look at that—and that—" He pointed to a bureau top and a table, both evenly spread with the light powder he had sprayed on them. "Not a mark! He wiped the place clean before he vamoosed. A pretty slick operator."

"I wonder," said Lance skeptically. "Naturally, when he discovered he'd lost a Band-Aid, he'd take ordinary precautions. Let's see if he's really smart or just run-of-the-mill."

"How do we do that?"

"We'll forget obvious surfaces like dressers and light-switches. Any fool would wipe those off."

"How about bathroom fixtures?"

"He'd think of those, too. The point is what wouldn't he think of."

"Radio dials?" suggested Ellis doubtfully.

"Let's jump into Benson's skin for a minute." This was a trick of Lance's which the men who worked with him knew well: identifying himself with the crook he was hunting, entering his mind, and registering what he would do or not do in any given circumstances. Unimaginative critics called the process flighty and out-of-place in a realistic police force but had to admit that he often got startling results. When this occurred, they called it "Wiley's Luck." Now he said, "Let's see. We're Benson. We're stopping in this room. We wake up in the morning, step into our slippers and reach for a bathrobe, maybe call Room Service for breakfast—" He grinned ruefully. "I'm a fine one, touching that phone. I ought to be walking a beat, slipping up there. Well, even if the horse is stolen, you better spray the phone, just in case." The sprayed phone showed a fine set of Lance's prints and nothing else, not even smudges. It, too, had been wiped clean. When this was disposed of, Lance went on: "Well, we've ordered breakfast. While we wait for it, we might as well shower and shave—" He snapped his fingers. "Come on, Ellis, we'll soon see how bright Mr. Benson is!"

He led the way to the bathroom, opened the door of the shower stall by pressing back the catch with the point of his knife and said, "Step inside, Ellis. Spray powder on all four walls of the shower on the inside. There isn't a man alive can take a shower without bracing himself with his hand against the glass at some point—while he's soaping a foot or—"

Ellis came up with a most beautiful print of an outspread left hand, all five fingers and even the palm, clear as day. He knew his work well and gave a whoop, "You got it, Chief! Same thumb!"

"Same old story." Lance nodded. "They're all foxy up to a point but I've yet to meet a really intelligent crook. This one's even below average."

"How do you figure that?"

"Well, would a really slick operator use a showy iris Cadillac on his jobs as he did in L.A.? Would he take a chance on striking eyebrows, no matter how pretty they made him? I think this boy's so in love with himself, he sacrifices safety to his own conceit." He broke off and added briskly, "Get that print down to CBI fast. They haven't come up with anything yet on the thumb print, but with the whole hand to work with, it ought to be easier."

He gave the room a comprehensive search for any illuminating papers or other dues but drew a blank.

Leaving Ellis to lift and photograph the print and any others he might find, Lance went back to 35th

Street. The pile of reports on his desk was now mountainous. Detailed reports of all Mack's connections, public and private, gave a complete picture of the dead man's life. An uncle and aunt, residing in Utah, were his only surviving relatives. His business associates had only admiration and affection for him. His "love-life" was scanty. His true mistress was music, and while he dated many girls, there was no one of them close enough to constitute a force either for love or hate.

Donald Tanner's statements were all corroborated. The Cleveland doorman, an august individual as impressive as a field-marshal, remembered Tanner dropping Mack at the door and driving away. The time had been 6:20. The garage-man stated that Tanner had brought his car in just before 6:30. The elevator man at Tanner's apartment house brought the alibi full circle: he had taken Tanner up around 6:30 and down again half an hour later.

The phone on Lance's desk rang. The operator said, "Lieutenant, would you talk to a man who thinks he can help you in the Mack case?"

"Would I! Put him on."

The man's name was Marron and he ran a used-car business on Long Island. He had heard the noon broadcast, hooking up Mack's murder with a Los Angeles killing and mentioning an iris Cadillac as being implicated.

"I bought one of those along about two, two and a half months ago and I thought you might be interested."

"I am. Do you have the exact date?"

"Sure. Right here on my desk. March 13th."

"And the owner's name?"

"Victor Clyde."

"Can you describe him?"

"Yes, I remember him real well for a couple of

reasons."

"Go on."

"Well, for one, we don't handle many iris Cadillacs. They're a little fancy for the suburban trade. Secondly, he gave up so easy. I named a price and not too liberal a one because I knew I'd have trouble moving an iris Caddy. He jumped at it. What's more he wanted cash—didn't want a check. Think he said he was leaving town—"

Lance controlled his impatience and said again, "Can you describe him?"

"Big fellow, maybe six feet but built in proportion. Around thirty, thirty-five. Nice-looking type but nothing special about him."

"Dark or light?"

"Brownish hair, what I could see of it."

"Then he wore a hat?"

"Yeah, I guess so. In fact, I'm sure he did."

"Pulled down in front?"

"N-no, not that I remember—"

"Well, could you see his eyebrows?"

"Eye— Hey, wait a minute—that's right! I did notice his eyebrows. They were special—sort of swept on, almost like make-up. You think they were a disguise?"

"Did they seem to be?"

"No. I can't say that. But if this guy's a murderer, wouldn't he be smart enough to do something about a thing like that if they were real?"

"Mr. Marron, I don't think he is very smart."

"Yeah, I get you." Marron laughed. "'You can't win.' Well, I hope I helped you."

"You have indeed, Mr. Marron. You've been most civic-minded and I'm grateful. You won't mind if I send a man out to talk a little further to you?"

"Not a bit. And my name's spelled M-a-r-r-o-n in case it gets into the papers."

"Right. And thanks again."

Five minutes later there was a message on the teletype to Los Angeles, asking them to broadcast for any local information about a man named Victor Clyde, description as given by Herman Grotz and driving an iris Cadillac.

Egan came in to announce a visitor: Roderick Camden, Vice-President of the TV network to which Lee Mack had been under contract. Mr. Camden, not nearly so impressive looking as the Cleveland doorman, explained his visit. The network had canceled its usual TV program from 8 to 9 p.m. that evening and was devoting the time to a special memorial in honor of Lee Mack. Outstanding musicians had volunteered to sing and play Mack melodies; the president of the network, Mack's collaborator, Donald Tanner, and several notable public figures would speak. Mr. Camden asked Lance to appear, making a short address from the police angle, assuring the public that everything possible would be done to find the murderer.

Lance objected.

"Mr. Camden," he said, pointing to the massive pile of reports on his desk, "my job is detecting, not speechmaking. I'm up to my neck in work. I approve of your memorial. Lee Mack certainly earned it. But I do not approve of the police sounding off to the public until we have something to sound off about. I'll talk when the murderer is in custody, not before."

Mr. Camden might not be impressive to look at but he carried powerful ammunition. He said gently, "The Commissioner feels differently, Lieutenant."

Lance stared at him, stopped in full flight. "The—?" he began.

Mr. Camden placed a memo on Lance's pile of reports. "As long as I was seeing you myself, Lieutenant, he suggested I bring along his recommendation in person."

Lance glanced at the terse "recommendation." It

was an unmistakable order.

"Very well, Mr. Camden," he said tight-lipped.

Mr. Camden smiled, still gently, and proceeded to give Lance time, place, advice, and guidance about the proposed speech. To the irritated Lance, Camden's final suggestion was the last straw: "Oh, one thing more. The president of the network feels that we should keep the level of the memorial high. To that end, he asks everyone who participates to dress in a manner that will do honor to Lee Mack. Not formal, you understand. But a dinner coat seems more in keeping with the occasion than mere workaday clothes."

When the door closed behind Camden, Lance ground his teeth in anger which was part stupefaction. How a dinner coat could add to the veneration and homage of the event was beyond him. But it had its good side. It was late afternoon. He would have to go home to Riverdale to change; he could have dinner with Meg and see Sandy before his bedtime. He hadn't seen Meg since early yesterday morning. Until the Mack crime had come in, he had been busy with the last touches on the East Side child murder which was now wrapped up. Except for a few hours' sleep at Headquarters, he had been working steadily for thirty-two hours. Even a few minutes with Meg and the boy would untwist the knots that were tightening in him. Before he left, he issued a few terse orders. Even if he himself had to waste several hours, he could delegate some of the necessary work while he was gone.

Half an hour later, he turned off the Parkway and drove west until he reached the steep little street which ran down to the river. It was a short street, only three houses on each side, but all with ample grounds. The district was the nearest thing to country life that one could have and still be conveniently close to a Manhattan job. As his car slid down to the last house on the left, the late afternoon sun sparkled on the Hudson and gilded the windows of his rosy brick ranch-type home. The knots untwisted fast. Meg's greeting finished the job, "Lance! This is pure gravy! I didn't think I'd see you all week."

He explained, adding with a sour grin, "So now there's a TV star in the family."

"Oh, darling, you must hate it," she said, not fooled by his flippancy. "But the network does have a point. There are millions—literally millions—of people worked up, outraged, furious at this horrible thing that's happened. Their first reaction is 'Do something about it!' Well, tell them you are doing something—"

"No! Let them leave me alone to do it, not blat about it. Look at the time I waste. Half an hour driving up here. Why? To tog myself out in a dinner coat. I wonder what they'd have done if I hadn't owned a dinner coat. Then another half hour to write and memorize a two-minute speech. More time wasted getting back to the TV studio, rehearsing the damn speech and lastly, waiting a full hour till my turn to spout. Do you realize the actual work I could be doing in that time?"

"And do you realize the actual good you'll be doing? Those millions of people need some comfort." She grinned at him. "They need a good-looking, forceful, determined man to stand up and tell them that he personally will see to it that Lee Mack's killer is caught."

"Maybe you'd better write the speech," he retorted acidly. But the tense lines in his face smoothed out as he caught her close. "And thanks for the good-looking, forceful, et cetera. How does it feel to be loved by such a paragon, Mrs. Wiley?"

"Darn nice. Even if it's by remote control most of the time."

At this point, Sandy clattered into the house,

looking suspiciously demure. Lance, knowing the look, eyed him and asked, "And what have you been up to, young Sandy?"

"Who? Me?" The blue eyes were much too innocent.

"Nobody else. Been breaking the law?"

"Not a very big one."

"Let's have it."

"Well, everybody's away—"

"Who's everybody?"

"The Mayos—the—everybody on the block. Account of the holiday. So what harm did I do using all the back yards as a runway for my space ship?"

"Hah! So the crime's trespassing."

Sandy cocked a knowing eye. "Well, it's not a felony. Just a misdemeanor. You said so." Artfully, he tried to create a diversion. "Want me to spell 'misdemeanor'?"

Meg intervened. "I want you to wash up. Dinner'll be early because Daddy has to leave soon."

"I'm perfectly clean. There's no dust in the stratosphere—"

"You heard me, Sandy. And, no! I don't want you to spell 'stratosphere'!"

Philosophically, Sandy went to the bathroom while Meg and Lance gave way to their chuckles.

"He's the greatest," Lance said softly. "Downtown, they talk about Wiley's Luck. They don't know the half of it."

CHAPTER EIGHTEEN

While Lance was reading reports, talking to Marron and Camden, Victor devoured the morning papers he had brought back from Manhattan. As it was borne in on him what a prominent and beloved figure Lee Mack was, he began to feel more than the usual pride which he always took in his exploits. This was no ordinary crime. He—Frankie Edwards—the kid from a dusty Ohio farm, had, single-handed, committed the outstanding crime of the century and had got away with it; and that in spite of a tremendous piece of bad luck—the loss of the Band-Aid. Well, much good it would do them, finding it and even the thumb print on the wallet. Where could they go from there? Exactly nowhere. Although it was pretty fast work of that Homicide dick connecting it up with the Grotz business, as they said on the radio. He turned again to page 2 of the paper which had published Lance's picture.

For a long time he stared at it, taking in the square chin and the steady eyes which, even in a notoriously disfiguring newspaper cut, came through with authority and force.

"Sucker!" he jeered.

But the pictured face made him restless. He gathered all the papers together and took them upstairs where he stowed them carefully in a drawer, like an actor preserving good notices. Then he took the peroxide he had bought that morning and applied it generously to his eyebrows. When it had dried, he examined them in the mirror. They were lighter but still had that springing sweep which made them such an outstanding feature. He rummaged through his toilet articles until he found a pair of tweezers and began to pull out hairs haphazardly. Then he stepped back and eyed the over-all result. The noticeable eyebrows were now perfectly ordinary. He was elated and yet resentful. Like a pettish child, he blamed Lance Wiley for spoiling his distinctive appearance.

The restlessness persisted. Lance Wiley nagged at him like a hangnail. The printed face was not enough. He had an urge to see the man in the flesh. He chuckled as he contemplated going down to Homicide East in Manhattan and hanging about until he caught a real look at Wiley. He gave up that idea as a bit fantastic but still the thought of Wiley stayed with him, dominating his thoughts and keeping him from settling down to anything. Jessie was in the kitchen, from which the delectable odor of baking cookies emanated.

On an impulse, he left the house and drove into the village. He told himself that his first and most natural move should be to look in on Hewitt's after a four-day absence. There were a few customers in the store but Orville Bayne turned and greeted him at once. Jubilantly, he reported a sharp increase in sales of air-conditioners and deep-freezes to the neighboring estates and villas, but Victor hardly listened. As soon as he could, he retreated to the glassed-in office and pulled the Manhattan phone book off its shelf. Hewitt's Farm and indeed Crawfey village *in toto* would have scorned to give a Manhattan phone book house-room. But a business could hardly be that insular.

There was no Lance Wiley in the Manhattan book. Victor was inordinately disappointed. He had no idea why he wanted to know Wiley's address and phone number. There may have been a subconscious compulsion to phone the Lieutenant from some neutral pay station, to jeer at him and identify himself just before hanging up; to take the cocksure look off Mister Lance Wiley's calm face.

He tried the Brooklyn book without result. He found what he wanted in the Bronx book. He noted the address and phone number, put the books back and emerged from the office. He went out to his car and for the second time that day, headed toward New York.

When he found Lance's street in Riverdale, he drove past, parked on the southbound avenue, and walked back. The little street was deserted. No one on the sidewalks, on the terraces, on the lawns. He walked the length of the street to the wall above the river, noting by the number that Lance Wiley's house was the last of the row on the left. He was nearly at the top of the street again, and about to return to his car when a small boy in a space-suit darted out of a backyard, buzzing like a rocket ship. As he reached the Wiley lawn, he pushed back the bulky headpiece and yelled, "Hey, Mommy, can I have some crackers? I'm starved."

In the quiet air, the words reached Victor. He turned his head enough to see the "spaceman" go up the steps of the last house on the left. Victor went on to his car. He told himself he was a fool, wasting gas to get a load of how a lousy cop lived in his two-bit house on his two bit salary.

His success with the eyebrow job gave him confidence. He drove on down to a Broadway subway station and bought early editions of the afternoon papers. He reached home again at about the time that Lance was explaining the Mack memorial business to Meg.

The afternoon papers carried the news of it. Victor congratulated himself on having bought the first TV set that Hewitt's had received. Nobody, he grinned to himself, would be a more attentive viewer that evening than he.

The moment Jessie saw him, she stared and exclaimed, "Vic! Your eyebrows!"

"Yeah. The damn things are making headlines. I thought I'd pipe 'em down a bit. Good job, baby?"

"Wonderful. But won't people—?"

"Orville never looked at me twice."

"But the women will."

"Well, when I'm going to be inspected by Nosy Parkers like Esther Wells, I'll use a little eyebrow pencil, and gradually taper off. But just now, it's a hell of a lot more important to have ordinary eyebrows. I should have done it long ago—as soon as

Grotz gave out with his description in L.A."

"We ought to have an excuse ready—you know—an accident with your cigarette-lighter—in case someone says something—"

"And call attention to them? Nix. Look, honey, for the last few weeks we've been away from here most of the time. People don't notice and remember for long. They're too busy trying to be noticed themselves. If anybody does look twice, they'll just think they were mistaken."

"But if the headlines—"

"Headlines in the Crawfey weekly rag about eyebrows? Don't make me laugh. With the Crawfey Fair coming up to spread themselves on?"

"The estate people read the New York papers and they come into the village often."

"Smart kid. I'll stick to Hewitt's Farm for a while."

"Wouldn't Harry Bell hear somehow?"

"He might. They send out flyers to every police station in big cases. And this one's sure big." He smiled jauntily. "But you know Harry. He'd shoot anybody who hinted that there could be a criminal in Crawfey. Especially a poker buddy of his. Forget it, baby. We're sitting pretty. Not a thing in the world to worry about."

"I know—but the whole thing's so awful—it just haunts me."

"Now cut that out. It's maudlin. I don't like it any more than you do." He reddened angrily. "It was all his own fault, the damned tightwad. Bucking me for a few lousy dollars. He asked for it and he got it. It's over. So don't go chicken on me. I thought you had more guts."

But at 8 p.m. Jessie had no stomach to watch the Mack memorial on TV. She pleaded a headache and went to bed. Victor was faintly miffed at her defection but as he sat in the darkened living room, watching the development of the impressive program, he lost himself in the magnitude of his own achievement.

The president of the network opened the proceedings with a eulogy to Lee Mack, as sincere as it was extravagant. Inevitably he quoted Andrew Fletcher of Saltoun about the maker of the nation's laws and the maker of its songs. He spoke of the delight which Mack's music and personal appearances had given to millions, and deplored that this precious gift had been annihilated by the dastardly shot of an assassin. With actual tears in his eyes, he announced that he could say no more; he would let Lee Mack's music speak for him.

A top-flight soprano from the Met then sang one of Mack's best known songs, "All's Right With The World," a lovely lilting melody, familiar to probably ninety per cent of the population. An officer of ASCAP and a representative of the Mayor spoke briefly but feelingly. Donald Tanner gave a moving portrait of Mack as coworker, friend and benefactor to unknown hundreds.

After a brilliant potpourri of Mack's compositions played by a famous symphony orchestra, the president of the network rose again, with a sheaf of telegrams and messages in his hand, which he read aloud. They ranged from inmates of penitentiaries whose lot had been lightened by Mack's music and appearances on TV, all the way up to a sincere expression of shock and sympathy from the White House.

Victor seemed to expand in his chair. He sat up straighter, his shoulders squared themselves, he cocked his chin at an arrogant angle. Every speech, every telegram, which glorified Mack, aggrandized Victor even more. If Mack was all they said of him, how much greater was Victor who, by skill, nerve and, above all, brains, had snuffed this wonder-boy out in a split second. This was greatness.

The president of the network introduced Lieutenant Lance Wiley. There was a quick long-shot of the two men on the platform. Then, as Lance went to the microphone, the camera came in to a close-up as he began to speak.

Victor, with parted lips and a gleam of excited relish in his eyes, sat forward. It only needed this to fill the cup of his satisfaction and self-importance to the brim. He stared at the large clear presentment of Lance's lean face with its steady eyes and firm lips, and slapped his knee at the exquisite supreme joke: he, Victor, was living, breathing and alert, while his opponent was a mere dingus at the front of a TV tube, about as dangerous to Victor as a puff of wind.

Lance began: "Ladies and gentlemen: Others tonight have expressed far better than I could, the grief and shock and loss caused by Lee Mack's murder. I did not know him except as all you millions across the nation knew him—as a magician, with the genius to make us forget our troubles for a happy hour. The destruction of such a gift is, of course, outrageous.

"But I am a cop. To me, the taking of any human life is the lowest, most bestial, act in the world. My life is dedicated to the trapping of murderers. At this very moment I should be at work, hunting for Lee Mack's killer. But they tell me that I should spare a few moments to bring you a slight measure of comfort in your sorrow. Here is my assurance to you: I cannot bring Lee Mack back to you but I can avenge him— And I will.

"It should not be too difficult. Why? Because the murderer is stupid. You will understand that I cannot go into details here and now, but this killer is even more stupid than most criminals. He has less brains, less cleverness, less know-how. All he has is a gun.

"And so, if it eases your grief any, I give you my

promise that I will not rest until Lee Mack's murderer is in custody. I am going straight from here back to my office, to work around the clock, if necessary, to make that promise good. Thank you."

Victor's eyes were suddenly suffused with blood. He was indeed seeing red, with a rage so violent, so frenzied, that the screen blurred before him and his buzzing ears heard nothing of the final musical selection on the program. Stung, he leaped from his chair, kicking it over in a tempest of fury against Lance Wiley.

"Stupid."

The word thundered through his brain, suffocated him with the pounding of his heart and shortened his breath to quick gasps. He had a bursting orgiastic urge to rush down to Homicide East, where Mister Lance Wiley was "working around the clock" and shoot him in his tracks. All he had was a gun, was it? He'd teach the bastard not to belittle Victor Clyde, or his gun. . . .

Without conscious thought, moving as if under hypnosis, he snatched his zippered bag from the closet and flung himself outside to his car. Once more that second-self of his was in complete control. The pleasant, smiling, friendly Victor, so free with money and help, had vanished. In his place was the unreasoning killer who had battered the young redhead in the Philadelphia hotel room because his vanity had been outraged.

He was already on the West Side Highway when his hot fury fell away, replaced by a much deadlier sardonic anger. If he killed Wiley, who would suffer? Not Wiley. He'd be dead and out of it. It would be Victor Clyde, the cop-killer, who would be mauled and beaten and broken before the final horror of the chair. What a fool he'd be to play into their hands. But he could make Wiley suffer by shooting up his home, killing his family, robbing him of his wife and kid and making a laughingstock of him, besides. Because with care and any break in the cards, he could get away with it easily in that lonely Riverdale section and sit back laughing while the smart lieutenant was hunting for him.

When he reached Riverdale, the little street where Wiley lived was deserted. There wasn't a light in any house until, coasting silently down the steep hill, he saw that a soft light shone from the Wiley living room. The faint sound of music reached him. He smiled. The Victor Clyde luck was holding. The music would drown any sounds he might make, breaking in. With the precision a long practice, he adjusted his Band-Aids and donned his mask. He walked up the cement driveway past the side of the house to the back door. In no time, he had the door open and moved through the dark kitchen toward the sound of the music.

Suddenly, he stopped dead. A grin, lost in the dark, widened his mouth. A great idea had come to him. Wiley had called him stupid before fifty million people. He had said that all Victor had was a gun. Well, he would show Wiley and the fifty million just how brilliant, how superior Victor Clyde was to this mouthy copper. Sure, any thug with a gun could kill. But Victor Clyde, with his brains and know-how, had a much smarter shot in his locker. The thing was there, ready to use. But it took a man like himself to see the possibilities, to make use of the material he had, to show Lance Wiley the excruciating refinements of revenge that followed the belittling of a genius like Victor Clyde. As he moved noiselessly through the dark kitchen, his plan full-grown in seconds, he tossed a smiling salute to Jessie's grandfather. He reached the living-room door.

In the split-second before he struck, Meg sensed rather than heard him and turned in time to catch a glimpse of him. But she had no time to utter a sound.

The butt of the gun came down and she crumpled to the floor. In a matter of minutes, her mouth was covered with adhesive tape and her hands and feet bound.

Unruffled, almost leisurely, he moved across the hall to the bedrooms, using his cigarette-lighter as a torch. The first room was empty but he found the object of his search in the second one. Sandy, curled into a comical ball, was sleeping the just sleep of a space-man after hours. He was scarcely awake when he found himself gagged, trussed-up and thrown onto the floor behind the front seat of the car. The one mitigating feature of this outrage was that Victor by-passed the living room on his way out, thus saving Sandy the horror of seeing his mother on the floor.

The "second-self" might have gone berserk earlier, but now he exhibited a shrewd caution. No parkways or main thoroughfares for him with the tricky freight he carried. He drove through a maze of secondary roads, bypaths and country lanes. With every passing mile, his injured pride healed and his self-confidence grew. During the first part of the trip, he had glanced back nervously every few moments at his prisoner. Now, nearing the sanctuary of Hewitt's Farm, he didn't trouble to turn his head.

Sandy, helpless and uncomfortable, half-smothered under an old trench coat, was paralyzed with fright. He was eight and a half years old and mature beyond his age. He had no callow ideas that this was an exciting game of cops and robbers. He knew it for exactly what it was: a kidnaping. And he knew too that of all criminals, kidnapers were the ones who never played fair. You could meet their demands, pay their enormous ransoms and in return, nine times out of ten, get back only the dead body of the kidnapee.

Lance and Meg had never "talked down" to Sandy. They discussed practically everything before him, and, if it was obscure to his childish mind, they did their best to enlighten and explain. The three were a closed corporation and the intimacy gave Sandy an intelligence and power of clear thinking unusual in a boy of his years.

After the first awful period of sheer terror, he swallowed hard behind the painful adhesive tape and doggedly conjured up his ambition and his dream: to be, some day, a capable adjutant to Lieutenant Wiley of Homicide. He asked himself, with heart-breaking courage, what his father would want him to do. He knew the answer well: observe, pick up every scrap of information you can about your kidnaper and where you are being taken; it may come in handy.

Sandy was lying on his back. He wriggled until his head was free of the trench coat. In the dim light, he got an impression of broad shoulders and dark abundant hair looming above him in the front seat. The man no longer wore the horrible false face which had bent over him in his bed, but, until he turned around, Sandy could not hope to see his features.

As regards where they were going, Sandy mentally kicked himself for being so panic-stricken that at first he had noticed nothing at all about their route. But he wasted little time over that. It was past and he could do nothing about it. But, though he had missed the early past of their journey, maybe he could salvage something about the middle or the end of it. With this in view, he began to inch his pinioned but supple little body slowly and painfully about until he was on his side, then on his stomach, and finally, with an immense effort, close enough against the back seat to use it as a lever. He scrambled to his knees, his eyes on a level with the car window, behind the broad back of the driver.

He saw little, even though there was moonlight enough to see by. He was in the country, that was for sure. Tall trees loomed black against the sky, both at the roadside and farther away. No houses. His breath quickened as they passed massive gates and tall walls. It was a district of estates. The houses, he reasoned, were set back, out of sight of the road. But was that any help? It could be Jersey, Long Island, or upper New York State.

Suddenly, his eyes popped. The lights of the car lit up a roadside sign. A word sprang out of the darkness at him. Before he could see more, the car made a sharp right turn, throwing him to the floor. Perhaps it was lucky that it did so, because seconds later, the car bumped to a stop and the man turned and looked at him. If Sandy had still been at the window. . . . He shivered.

The man got out of the car, swathed Sandy's head in the trench coat so that he could see nothing and carried him into a house. They went down a flight of stairs. Sandy was laid, none too gently, on a cold, hard floor (he still had only pajamas on) while the man made small mysterious noises. Then, still blinded by the trench coat, Sandy was carried down another flight of stairs, thrown on a couch, and the trench coat was removed. He had caught just a flashing glimpse of the man's face when a voice far above drove him out of eyeshot.

"Vic! What are you doing down there?"

The man strode across the room.

"Nothing! Go back to bed!" he rasped.

The anxious voice, far from obeying, came nearer. "Is something wrong?"

Sandy, unobserved, dared to turn his head. The man was standing at the foot of a short flight of steps with a square hole at the top of them. He spoke savagely, "You heard me! Go back upstairs!"

"But why are you in Grandfather's den? Have they—traced you?"

"No! No! Damn it to hell, Jessie—"

A pair of feminine feet appeared on the top step.

"Vic! Stop trying to shut me out. If something's wrong—"

She was down the steps and had full view of the room. As her eyes lit on Sandy, she gasped, "What's this?"

The man gave a strident crowing laugh.

"Nothing. Just teaching 'em a lesson."

"Vic! You must be mad. You can't get away with a thing like this—"

"I can get away with anything."

She laid a soothing hand on his sleeve.

"Now, listen, darling. We're in trouble enough. The only way we can hope to dodge them is to lead our ordinary life and melt into the landscape. Why on earth did you do it?"

"You didn't hear him—" he barked.

"Hear who?"

"That bastard Wiley—sounding off—"

"You mean this is—?" She gasped again.

"Right the first time. I'll teach him what I can do."

"But Vic, think of us. Living here in a little village. We can't hope to keep it a secret—"

He gave the crowing laugh again.

"No? Why not, with this snug little hidey-hole?"

"But a child—! Oh, Vic."

"Now you listen to me," he said angrily. "You sound like I'm some kind of a brute, planning to torture the kid. All I'm doing is giving Mister Lieutenant Wiley a little lesson. You know what he called me—me—?"

"I don't care, Vic! I only care about keeping you safe and out of their clutches. Look, darling. It's not too late. Take him back—"

"It is too late. Get a load of him, eating up every word we've said. And he's had a good gander at both of us. It's more dangerous now to let him go than to keep him."

"But you have to do it sometime—"

"We'll cross that bridge when we come to it," he said sullenly. "Get this! He's here—and he's staying here till Wiley sweats blood." His tone suddenly became wheedling, endearing: "Look, honey, sure we can pull it off together. I'll stick close to the house and you tell people I've got the flu or something. Nobody'll come snooping. Even if they did, they couldn't find a thing. This room was built forty—fifty years ago. I bet there's not a soul in town knows it exists."

"But it was so unnecessary, Vic—"

"You didn't hear him."

"What could he say to lead you to such a wild—?"

"All right. All right," he blustered. "Maybe I lost my lead. Maybe I went crazy for a minute. Well, it's done. So stick with it."

He was ill at ease under her reproachful eyes. For something to do, he pulled out a cigarette and his lighter, the same lighter he had used as a torch in Lance Wiley's house. It was burnt-out and as he snapped it, only the spark from the flint rewarded him. Feverishly, he spun it again and again, as if it were the most urgent thing in the world to produce a flame. After a dozen futile tries, he flung it on the floor with a rage out of all proportion to its importance. Jessie's eyes changed. The protest and blame disappeared. A look of concern and compassion softened them. She slipped her arm through his and said softly, "Darling, you're dog-tired. You've got to rest."

It was true enough. He had driven about three hundred miles since morning, he had undergone a series of acute tensions in the last thirty hours, from the killing of Lee Mack to the atrocity at Lance's house. Above all, his insensate fury at Lance's TV speech had frayed his nerves and depleted his strength, both mental and physical, to an unbelievable degree. He wanted to sink into a chair or a bed and it would have taken very little to make him burst into maudlin tears. Jessie pushed him gently toward the steps leading up to the cellar, murmuring, "Leave everything to me. Just go and rest. I'll take care of it all. Will you do that, Vic?"

He went willingly enough, but at the top of the steps he gathered up a last spark of energy. He grasped her arm and spoke sharply: "You swear you won't double cross me?"

"Vic!"

"If you let that kid go, it's the chair for me."

She nodded.

"Then promise."

"I promise, Vic. You shouldn't have to ask. Now go. We'll talk when you feel better."

"That's my girl," he said, satisfied. Then a scrap of caution made him add in a whisper, "And when you come up, honey, pull something over the trapdoor so he can't lift it. There's a carton in the cellar—"

"Yes, Vic. Go now."

His footsteps retreated and Jessie returned to the den. She rummaged in a drawer of the workbench and brought out a pair of shears. She came over to Sandy and clipped the tape from his wrists and ankles. Her hair was disheveled and she looked distracted. Her lips were trembling uncontrollably but she ignored that, as if by refusing to admit fear, she could shut it out. Sandy understood that kind of defiance; it was one of his own traits. She said, "This is going to hurt. But a minute's hurt is better than being gagged, isn't it?"

Sandy batted his eyes in agreement. He was doing his best to hold back the tears of pain as the blood rushed into his hands and feet after their confinement. She took hold of a corner of the tape on his cheek and gave a quick jerk. It felt like fire and the tears did come now. But he ground his teeth together and somehow that kept the tears from rolling down. After a little, the pain got less. His lips felt swollen and stiff and hot, but every second it was better. They were silent for a few moments, eyeing each other. Then Jessie said, "Are you hungry?" He shook his head. She tried again, "What's your name?"

"Sandy," he croaked. And suddenly, they both giggled, ostensibly at the funny sound of his voice, actually as an outlet to ease the hysteria which had been building up in both of them. She leaned forward and slipped her arm around his shoulders.

"Sandy, don't be frightened. Nothing bad will happen to you."

He worked his lips to see if they were usable. They were. They still hurt but they were getting back to normal. He sat up and spoke earnestly, as if to someone of his own age, "I am frightened. And you better be, too. He's bad."

"No, he isn't. He does some bad things, I admit. But he wouldn't hurt me. And I won't let him hurt you."

"Didn't he ever hurt you?"

"Never. Never. He's the only person in the whole world who was ever good to me."

"But he does awful things."

"I—know," she whispered. "But . . . even so . . ."

"Now, you listen to me. If you're so sure he won't hurt you, tell you what you do. You let me go. I'll tell people I—I walked in my sleep—or curled up in somebody's car—I'll never tell he kidnaped me or who he is—" Her fingers tightened on his shoulder.

"You know who he is?"

"Sure I do. He's the one who killed Lee Mack. Mommy let me watch the memorial show because Daddy made a speech. Didn't you listen?" She shook her head. "Well, Daddy said some mean things about him—about how he was stupid—so for spite, he kidnaped me. He said so himself. You heard him."

"Yes." She rose uneasily, unwilling to face this evaluation of Victor. "It's late. We won't talk anymore now. I'll get you some sheets and a pillow."

"We better talk now. Tomorrow might be too late."

"What do you mean?"

Now he spoke as if she were considerably younger than he: "My Daddy is a lieutenant at Homicide. I know all about such things. Policemen get wild if anything happens to one of them or their kids. They never give up. And the FBI comes in when it's a kidnaping. Well, nobody ever gets the best of the FBI. You know that, don't you?" She shivered. "You don't have to do a thing. Just go up for the sheets. And when you come back, you'll find I've snuck out through that trapdoor and I'm gone."

She stood twisting her fingers, torn and defenseless, and then spoke desperately, "Sandy, I promised him. I swore I wouldn't double-cross him. He said it would mean the—chair."

His eyes sparked with anger. He spoke as Lance Wiley's son: "He deserves the chair. And you're just as bad if you help him."

She twisted her fingers in her hair. "Don't! I can't go back on him—no matter what he is. You don't understand. You're only a little boy—"

"You're just awful." His voice trembled. He was only a little boy, a badly frightened one. "He'll—he'll kill me and you won't do a thing to stop him."

"No, Sandy. I'll make you a promise, too. I swear I won't let him hurt you, let alone kill you. Is that all right?"

He stared at her doubtfully. He didn't quite believe her but at least he wasn't afraid of her. And the man had gone away when she asked him to. Maybe she could talk him out of doing anything terrible.

"Well—" he said uncertainly.

"Now I'll go and get the sheets," she said briskly, enormously relieved. "I'll be back in a few minutes."

She ran up the stairs and he noticed bitterly that she closed the trapdoor after her. His heart sank. That showed him where she stood. She might sound kind and friendly but she was on the man's side the whole way. Sandy couldn't count on her for any help. He would have to trust himself; make up some kind of a plan to escape in spite of them both.

But his heart sank as he looked around the old-fashioned, rather cozy little room. One horrible fact stood out: there were no windows; the trapdoor was the only exit. And he noticed that when it was closed, he couldn't hear a sound from the cellar above. That meant that yelling would do him no good, even if an outsider was in the house to hear it. Barefooted, he ran up the steps and examined the underside of the trapdoor. It was innocent of handle, lock, or keyhole. He pushed at it hard but it didn't budge. It simply did not occur to him that pressure on a certain spot would release a spring which, in turn, would cause the door to rise. He accepted it as a horrid fact that it could not be opened from below. The future aide to Lieutenant Wiley, of Homicide, was still green.

A claustrophobic terror swept over him: he was boxed in the room. Maybe that talk about sheets was just hooey. She had dropped the trapdoor and gone back to the man, leaving Sandy there forever. Slowly he dragged himself down the steps. He clutched at his last remaining stand-by in time of trouble: what would Lieutenant Wiley do? This wasn't like the usual made-up problems he and Daddy played in the Game, the detective Game where there was a definite clue and a solution which entitled the winner to say with pseudo-modesty: "It just takes brains." This was like one of the tricky ones that Daddy now and then slipped into the Game and Sandy had to say, "I give up" and Daddy answered sternly, "Wrong. You don't ever 'give up.' You mark it 'Case unsolved. Still open.'"

His little jaw set. There was a quaver in his voice but it was loud: "Case unsolved. Still open."

A few minutes later, the trapdoor swung back silently and Jessie came down, her arms bulging with bedclothes. She fixed up the wide couch with sheets and a summer blanket, slipped a pillow deftly into its case and then held out a pair of red knitted bedroom slippers with a friendly smile.

"Try these. I bet my feet aren't much bigger than yours."

As he tried them on, he couldn't for the life of him help laughing. The slippers were too small. Jessie laughed, too, and used the shears to snip a hole in each toe.

"Now you're really in style," she said. "Open-toes are the thing." Then she did something that very nearly wiped out all his resentment against her. She handed him a flashlight. "The light-switch down here is at the top of the steps. If you have to go to the bathroom, it's easier to use a torch."

"Bathroom?" His voice rose hopefully. "Where's that?"

"In that little cubby-hole over there."

"Oh." His voice dropped heavily. But his inbred politeness persisted. "Well, thanks anyway. I'll make out okay."

"Yes." Her fingers ran through the mop of his tawny hair. "Don't worry about anything. Just go to sleep. It's late."

"It's not my fault it's late," he flashed back.

Like lightning, the friendly face before him changed to a haunted mask.

Sandy thought, "She's even so scareder than I am."

She whispered good night, ran up the stairs,

clicked off the light and was gone. Sandy turned on the flashlight and directed its ray upward. The trapdoor was firmly in place.

CHAPTER NINETEEN

The moment the telecast was over, Lance left the studio. By 9:30 he was back in his office. Sergeant Knight, after a few hours' sleep, was on the job again. He greeted Lance exuberantly: "Things been bustin' out all over. We're on our way."

"Let's have it." Lance's eyes sparkled with interest.

"Well, first, CBI didn't have a thing on those prints Ellis lifted from the stall shower in Benson's room, so we hustled them over the Speedphoto Transceiver to Washington. They came up with the answer fast. Benson may be Victor Clyde now and then, but he was drafted into the Army as Francis Edwards, of Alma, Ohio, back in 1944. He's thirty-two as of now."

"Good work. Did you contact Alma?"

"Yes. The father still works a farm outside the town. The Police Chief says he'll investigate."

"The Chief co-operative?"

"Yeah, very obliging. They liked Lee Mack in Alma, too."

"Maybe he'll stake out a plant at the father's farm. When Edwards realizes this is a nation-wide manhunt, he may run to cover there."

"I'll get it on the teletype."

"Did you give any of this to the press boys?"

"No, sir. I left that to you."

"Good. We'll keep that dark a while. What else?"

"You left orders to canvass the big hotels for Victor Clyde, between March eighth and March thirteenth."

"Yes, I did. As soon as Marron phoned in about buying an iris Cadillac here in town from Clyde on the thirteenth."

"Goldman found him. He registered at the Commodore on March twelfth. With a dame. Mr. and Mrs. Victor Clyde. Checked out on the fifteenth."

"Let's see. Grotz is held up on the seventh. Dies on the eighth. Clyde-Edwards lams out of town in the Caddy. Arrives here on the twelfth. Sells the car on the thirteenth. So the Cadillac's a washout as a clue. Probably driving a sky-blue Chrysler or a fireman-red Ford by now."

"Nope. Goldman's a good man. He didn't leave it at that. He ferreted out the bellhop who brought him in and the one who helped him leave."

"Way back in March?"

"He had a piece of luck on both ends. When he arrived, Clyde left his Caddy before the door while they took up his luggage. They had to call him from the desk to come down and take it away and the kid offered to drive it to a garage for him. He refused but the incident stuck in the kid's head because he's auto-minded and wanted to get behind a Caddy wheel."

"And at the other end?"

"The dame helped out on that. While the second bellhop was loading the stuff into the car, he heard her say: 'Vic, where's the Cadillac?' This kid didn't know what car they arrived in, so it didn't mean much to him but he did remember that much when Goldman prodded him."

"Did he remember what car they went off in?"

"Only that it was black."

"That's a help," said Lance grimly.

"Well, it saves us scouting after iris Cadillacs."

"Marron did that for us. Did any of the other boys come up with a Victor Clyde at another hotel?"

"No."

"Then he's switching names every time he registers. Dead end. Dave, I want a photostat of his registration card from the Commodore and the Cleveland. I want a man on the big hotels till Clyde registers somewhere again. No matter what the name, the same handwriting will be there."

"Will do. But if he scoots out of town?"

"If the Alma police can't cover the father's farm around the clock, we'll send our own men out."

"There's a good few other places in the U.S."

"I'm getting a man from Special Services to draw a composite. Hastings, of the Cleveland, remembers Clyde clearly and can give him tips on contour, bone-structure or whatever, until he gets a fair likeness. The eyebrows'll help a lot. Then we publish it in the press from coast to coast."

"Swell. Samson's the man. We brought in the Shetland murderer with one of his drawings. Remember?"

"Yes. Anything else?"

"That's about all." Knight sounded let-down, discouraged. "For a minute there, I figured we had it made. But unless Edwards connects with his father, I guess we're no for'rarder than we were."

"Of course we are." He clapped the Sergeant on the shoulder. "You ever hear of a kid joining up who didn't have his picture taken for the family to set out on the parlor table? Even an old photo's better than a description. Add a request for one on the Alma teletype."

"I'll do that," Knight said, regalvanized.

Lance turned to the mountain of reports on his desk. It was almost unbelievable how much had accumulated since five o'clock when he had gone home to change into his dinner coat. A dozen individuals had phoned in that "Benson" was holed up across the street or upstairs from them. The radio and TV newscasters had circulated what was known of Victor's appearance at Lance's instigation. He considered the public willing and effective legmen, whose co-operation often aided the police immensely. Of course there were cranks and well-meaning but wrong-headed people who would flood Headquarters with tips, all of which had to be investigated and nearly all of which would be futile. But among the hundreds of useless pointers, there might be one which would show the way to the criminal.

After a solid hour's reading, Lance glanced at his watch. It was four minutes past eleven. A little late for his usual eleven o'clock call to Meg. He asked the board for his home number. He heard the buzz at the other end sound half a dozen times before the switchboard operator said, "Don't seem to answer, Lieutenant."

"Okay. I'll try again later."

He frowned a little but he was not really worried. Meg was probably in the shower, although in ten years of married life, the quarter hour from 11 to 11:15 was religiously kept free and clear for Lance's call unless it was understood beforehand that the call would not be coming through. Lance snapped his fingers. Of course! She didn't expect his call; on television, he had already informed her (as well as millions of others) that he was going from the studio right to his office to work "round the clock if necessary." He went back to the reports.

But he was not giving them his undivided attention. A mouse of doubt was nibbling at his consciousness. Meg was something of a night-owl. Twelve, even one o'clock, seemed to her a civilized bedtime. He could picture her, curled on the living-room couch, reading or listening to records, sometimes even sketching. She had an undeveloped knack for drawing which ran in her family; the Hatfields were all more or less artistic. Her brother, Martin, had parlayed the gift into a magnificent income as a commercial artist.

At twenty minutes past eleven, the "mouse" was definitely interfering with his efficiency. He asked again for his number. This time he let it ring twelve times before he hung up slowly. He considered. If Meg had been in the shower at 11:04, she would have been out of it at 11:20. If she had, for once, gone to bed early, she would still have awakened and answered his call. She was a light sleeper, like all mothers, and she couldn't be out. It would take a major calamity for her to leave Sandy alone in the house for even five minutes.

At 11:25, he asked for another Riverdale number. Four blocks from his house, Meg's brother, Martin Hatfield, lived in a near-castle, far more imposing than the Wileys' modest home. Lance's relief was out of all proportion to the situation, when his brother-in-law came to the phone.

"Hello, Marty. Lance. Am I disturbing you?"

"Not a bit. Penny and I are watching the late show. And is it a stinker! What's on your mind?"

"Well, look. I've been calling Meg for half an hour and I can't raise her. I don't want to act jittery but—"

"Jittery! Why not? Meg'd rather miss an Inauguration Ball than your eleven o'clock call. I'll shoot over there in the Jag and call you right back. Okay?"

"Swell. And thanks a lot, Marty."

Ten minutes later, Lance's phone rang. It was Marty but Lance could hardly recognize his usual debonair tones in the choppy husky voice: "Lance. Get up here fast."

"What's wrong?"

"Don't ask. Get here." He hung up in Lance's ear.

When Lance raced up the walk and into his house, the first person he saw was Dr. Egbert, their family physician, kneeling beside someone on the floor. Behind him, Marty had his arm around his weeping wife, Penny. Lance pushed past them. Dr. Egbert was ripping adhesive tape from Meg's mouth. Then he slashed the bonds which tied her hands and feet. She didn't wince. Lance uttered a strangled cry.

"Is she—?"

"She's breathing. But unconscious. Leave her to me. You'd better talk to Hatfield—"

Lance turned and faced Marty. "What's he mean—?" He caught his breath. "Sandy—?"

Penny sobbed, "He's gone! Oh, Lance—"

Lance rushed into Sandy's room, saw the tumbled bed, the clippings of adhesive tape. He died a little.

Fifteen minutes later, Meg's eyelashes fluttered. Dr. Egbert said softly, "I'll ring for an ambulance—"

Meg spoke faintly but positively: "No. I want to be here."

"Meg, darling—"

"Lance—he wore a Hallowe'en mask—" Her eyes closed.

Lance scooped her gently into his arms and carried her to their bedroom. Within half an hour, a nurse had been installed and Meg was sleeping under a light sedative. Dr. Egbert was replacing the paraphernalia in his bag.

"You're lucky," he told Lance. "Her thick hair saved her. There's a slight concussion but it's nothing to worry about. By morning she should be nearly normal. I don't have to tell you to keep the news about the boy from her. Any shock—"

"We keep that news from everybody." Lance, seemingly stupefied up to now, came suddenly to life. His eye ranged from the doctor to Marty, Penny, and the nurse. "I know who did this and the only chance of getting Sandy back is complete secrecy. Marty, you and Penny go home and behave exactly as usual—"

"I'm not leaving Meg alone in the house with just a nurse—"

"In half an hour, there'll be a police guard on the

house, front and back. I'll wait till they get here."

"Well, all right, then—" He and Penny left with the doctor. Lance got into action on the phone. He called his office and asked for Sergeant Knight.

"Dave, did you get that teletype out to Alma?"

Knight was flustered.

"I didn't, Lance. A bar-and-grill knifing came in before I got around to it—I'll get on to it right away—"

"No. Get the Alma Police Chief on the phone instead. Impress it on him not to give it to the press— about Edwards' father—it's important—"

"Okay. What's up?"

"Later. Phone right away. I'll be down soon."

"Should the Alma end still stake out the farm?"

"Yes. But on the quiet. No publicity." He hung up, jiggled the phone, asked to be connected with the squad-room and arranged for the stakeout on his own house. When the men arrived, Lance explained to a limited extent to them, looked in on Meg who was sleeping naturally, arranged with the nurse to call his office every hour, and left in his car.

On his way downtown, he stopped at an apartment house on East Seventy-ninth Street. On the way up in the elevator, he looked at his watch. It was 1:46. He rang the bell. After not too long a wait, the door opened and a gray-haired man in pajamas and robe confronted him. He was flushed with sleep but at sight of Lance, his eyes were instantly alert. He was Captain Richard Manders, Lance's immediate superior. No surprise, no annoyance, no censure showed in him as he led the way to a small study.

"Tell it," he said quietly. He knew Lance well and knew that if Lance rang his bell at such an hour, there was good and sufficient reason for it.

Lance told it all: from the leads to Victor Clyde, who was actually Francis Edwards, to the attack on Meg and the kidnaping of Sandy.

"What do you want?" Manders asked at the end of it.

"Secrecy. I want the story about Sandy kept dark."

"Why?"

"The man's a maniac."

"Pretty shrewd maniac up to now, to my thinking."

"Foxy, yes. But swollen with ego, like all of them." Lance dashed his hand across his face. "I blame myself for this, Chief. They rang me in on that memorial service for Mack and I said too much. I called Edwards stupid and a few other things—I was about as nasty as they let you get on TV."

The Captain brushed this aside.

"What good will secrecy do? A man with an eight-year-old boy in tow isn't easy to hide. The public's help is our best bet."

"Not yet."

Manders gave him a steady look. He didn't mince words.

"You know how dangerous delay is in these cases. Give him enough time to find the boy a liability and he'll dispose of him."

Lance answered through set jaws, "Oh, God, I do. He may have done it already. But if he hasn't, he may be on his way to his father's farm to hide out. The place will be covered before he can arrive."

"I see your point. But if he doesn't make for the farm?" Manders asked, just as Knight had done.

"Then this: if there's not a syllable in the papers about his great coup of snatching the son of the man who's hunting him down, he'll feel cheated."

"So?"

"He'll do something about it."

"Yes, I think he will," Manders said grimly.

In his urgency, Lance resorted to his old habit of getting into the skin of the man he was hunting.

He spoke earnestly: "Put it like this, Chief: I'm a holdup man. Not a killer unless I have to be. Only in a tight corner. I pull a dozen jobs and the cops never get close. No record. I begin to think I'm invulnerable. I kill Grotz and get away with that too. I come east and go right on with my racket. I laugh in the cops' faces. I'm God's older brother. Then I tangle with Lee Mack, the darling of the country. It's splashed all over the papers. I eat it up. I'm the Master Mind, Public Enemy Number One, Mr. Brain. The papers, the cops, the public, talk of nobody but ME. Great! Then this lousy cop Wiley goes on television and punctures my puffed-up ego. Calls me stupid. ME. I go wild. I'll show him who's got brains! I'll hit him where it hurts. So I steal his kid right from under his nose. He'll be laughed off the force. And tomorrow's headlines about me will be bigger and better. I can't wait to see the papers. Tomorrow comes. I look and look. Not a word about the kidnaping. What the hell goes? I buy the evening papers. Still nothing. The bastards! But wait a minute—maybe they don't know that Mack's killer is the one who snatched the kid. Sure. That's it. Well, I'll put 'em wise. I'll call Wiley himself on the phone and laugh in his ear. Or send him a note. That'll put me right back on the front page." Lance dropped his impersonation. "Chief, I know the type. It's a chance for a lead. I'll have my phones—home and office— monitored so that every call I get will be traced as soon as I say 'hello.' Or if it's a letter, we'll have something to work on—"

There was a long pause. Then Manders spoke, moderately but unconvinced: "You Princeton boys who come into police work carry this psychiatric stuff too far, Lance."

"It's my boy," said Lance with difficulty.

Manders looked away.

"It's an awful risk, son," he said finally. "That

splendid little kid—" He had met Sandy a few times and had been charmed by him.

Lance gritted his teeth.

"It's my only chance. I myself don't think too much of the Ohio lead. Plums just don't fall into our mouths like that. And if he doesn't go home, he can be anywhere and we don't have a clue where. This way, we might get something—"

"There's the FBI to inform."

"That's okay. I don't care if every cop in America knows unofficially. I just want to insure that there's no leak to the papers. It's the only way I can think of to make Edwards show his hand." His voice went up half an octave in desperation. "Good God, Chief, this is my kid, the biggest thing in Meg's life and mine. Give me forty-eight hours. It's a risk either way. But there's a chance my way."

Reluctantly, Captain Manders gave in.

CHAPTER TWENTY

To his shame, Sandy slept soundly after the disturbing events of the night. He wakened only when Jessie came down the steps with a breakfast tray. The sight and smell of crisp bacon, eggs, oatmeal and milk were too much for a healthy boy, and Jessie watched the food vanish with approval. But as she began to stack the empty dishes on the tray, a sense of his predicament came over him in a wave. He looked past her, wondering if he could make a break for it, dash up the steps to the open trapdoor and out to freedom. His thoughts were mirrored in his candid face. She said, "Don't try it, Sandy. Even if you made it, you'd never get past him. And it might make him— ugly."

She stooped and gave him an unexpected kiss. He was suddenly terribly homesick and forlorn. It was all he could do to keep from throwing himself into her arms and pouring out his terror and misery. And that was a fine thing for a kidnapee to do with his kidnaper! He bit his lips to stop their trembling and managed to say severely, "I'm s'posed to have a bath."

"I'll bring down soap and towels and a wash cloth. But I haven't got a loose bathtub."

Now he had to bite his lip to keep from grinning. Her hair was dark while Mommy's was golden, but there was something alike about them—the way they joked and a sort of comfortableness. For the life of him, he couldn't hate her. She went on casually as if he were a mere visitor: "You play checkers?" He nodded. "I'll bring down the board after I do my chores. I'm pretty good at it. We'll play for a cookie a game."

After she was gone and the trapdoor closed, Sandy investigated the den. The drawers of the workbench were full of tools, some of them heavy enough to double as weapons. But Sandy was no cocky fool. He knew that even with a weapon, an eight-year-old boy was no match for an adult. He could not hide a wrench in his shallow pajama pocket, and if he had to reach for it before he struck, she would be on to him in time to stop him. And there was always the horrible man upstairs to reckon with, if he ever got that far. Sandy shied away from thoughts of the man; it sapped what little courage he had left.

He took a metal ruler and knocked against the walls of his prison with it. Solid cement. No hollow space, no panel with a secret exit behind it, as in the best books of adventure. There were some chisels and a hammer in the drawer. He might chip the cement and eventually make a hole big enough to wriggle through. But he was more mature than the average boy and he thought the plan through to its logical conclusion. He had been carried last night down two flights of stairs—(A) to the cellar, (B) to the den. Even cellars were built partly below ground, so certainly this sub-cellar was. If he made the hole, he would only strike earth and would then have to bore upwards for many feet to reach the outside air. That meant hiding the dirt he scooped away and masking the hole from his captors. He might do that all right—push a chair in front of the hole and deposit the dirt in the little booth where the toilet was. But suppose he did it. He glanced up at the ceiling. The room was about ten feet high, he figured. Add a few feet more for the part of the cellar that was below ground. Maybe thirteen feet in all. Say he managed to dig his way up four or five feet. After that, what? There was no ladder in the room and only two chairs. He could never dig much higher than his own head. The tunnel idea was out. He would have to work on Jessie, win her over to his side or trick her into a careless move.

Upstairs Jessie was indeed doing her ineffectual best for him. As she came up into the kitchen with Sandy's empty tray, Victor was just finishing his breakfast. She said, "He didn't leave a crumb. It's a pleasure to watch him stoking away."

Victor frowned. A night's sleep had restored him to his hearty bold-faced self. The sheepishness and self-justification of last night were gone. He was master here and it was a good time to emphasize it. He set down his cup.

"That's enough of the soft stuff."

"Oh, Vic, I didn't mean anything. But he is a cute little fellow—"

He pushed back his chair, rose and faced her.

"You sound like you don't have good sense. That brat isn't here on a week-end visit, you know. This is a kidnaping. Ever hear of the Lindbergh Law? If we're caught, it's the chair—for you and me both."

"Me?"

"Sure. You. Remember the Greenlease case? The woman got it right along with the man."

"But they—" She could not finish.

"That's right. They killed the kid—"

She grasped his arm and spoke hysterically, "Vic—Vic—please—please—let him go—tonight after dark—drive him over to Jersey—anywhere—set him down—he'll never be able to tell them—before it's too late—"

He smiled suddenly at her.

"Sure, honey. That's the program. But not just yet. We'll let Lance Wiley stew in his own juice for a while. Let him find out who's stupid."

"Oh, Vic, why should you care what he said—?"

"That's my business," he said in a hard tone. "Yours is to see the kid stays hidden till I'm sweet and ready to let him go." He dug his fingertips into her shoulders. "Now cut the cackle. Just remember your promise—you swore not to double-cross me—"

"I won't, Vic. I swear it again."

"Okay. I'm driving to town now to get the papers. I'm trusting you."

"And I'm trusting you. You'll surely let him go in a day or two?"

"Right." He laughed. "Want me to swear, too?"

She kissed him frenetically.

"Vic, I'm so glad. These awful things—one after another. Oh, I know Lee Mack wasn't your fault—it was self-preservation—but this—it wasn't like you—you must have been out of your mind—"

"Well, the truth is," he improvised easily, "I had a couple of drinks too many—I didn't know what I was doing."

Her face cleared. As he drove out of the garage, she was even humming over the breakfast dishes. She remembered to take soap and towels down to Sandy and he stretched a piecemeal bath into nearly an hour while she straightened the house. When she came down the second time with the checkerboard, she was buoyant. Until Victor's promise, she had not consciously realized what vague horrors lurked in her mind. She was so brimming with relief that she shared it with Sandy.

"Everything's all right," she told him. "You'll be going home soon now."

"He say so?"

"Yes, he promised." She opened the checkerboard. "Which do you want—red or black?"

Sandy, future aide to Lieutenant Wiley, looked at her cheerful face with some contempt. He was far from believing as wholeheartedly as she in Victor's promise. The checker game passed the morning pleasantly, although it precluded both thought and action toward escape. When she left him to prepare lunch, she still had his well-being in mind. "Sandy, do you like to read? I have a lot of my old books in the attic."

"Do you have a dictionary?"

"Dictionary?" She stared.

"Yes. I'm interested in spelling words. Tough ones."

"Oh. Well. Yes, I'm sure there's one. I'll bring it down with your lunch."

Sandy spent a cheerful afternoon, starting with the "A's." After all, a boy couldn't be expected to concentrate steadily on escape or the peril of his position, especially when his jailer, Jessie, was so friendly. He had not seen Victor at all today, so it was easy (and a lot more comfortable) to close his mind to his fear of him. And maybe it was true that Victor was going to let him go, as Jessie said. Wishful thinking is not too difficult when you are eight and a half.

Victor, meanwhile, drove down to New York as fast as the law allowed. His eagerness to see the morning papers was so great that he nearly stopped at one of the Westchester railroad stations on the way. But then he remembered that the suburban edition was shipped out early and would hardly contain news of a crime committed shortly before 11 p.m. and possibly not discovered until an hour or two later. What he wanted was the metropolitan edition with flaring headlines and maybe a stop-box on the front page. And for good measure news that Lieutenant Lance Wiley was prostrated with grief.

Fordham Road was busy enough to be safe, so he stopped there and bought all the papers at the subway station. This time he couldn't wait until he arrived back in Crawfey to devour them. He drove until he came to a cafeteria, found a free space in a parking-meter area, dropped in his dime, gathered up his papers and went in.

His coffee cooled before him as he scanned one after the other. His expression changed from relish to puzzlement to petulance to rage. Not a syllable about the kidnaping. It wasn't possible. What the hell did it mean? Then his face cleared and his smile came out like the sun from behind a cloud. Of course. Wiley said he was going to work around the clock. His wife hadn't been discovered in time for even the city editions.

But the evening papers would carry it. No sense in driving back to Crawfey and then trekking down again. It was 1:30 now. He would idle the time away until five, pick them up and get home before dinner. He went to the counter, picked up a sandwich and another cup of coffee, came back to his table and spent an hour over the papers again. If Sandy had been ignored in the news, Lee Mack was not. There was plenty about him—and correspondingly, from his point of view, plenty about Victor. He read with mixed feelings that Christopher Olsen, superintendent of a Los Angeles court apartment house, had come forward as soon as the name Victor Clyde had appeared in the news. Until then, he had not connected his prosperous, respectable, agreeable tenant with the wanted Cadillac or with crime. Mr. Olsen was suitably shocked and expressed willingness to come east at any time to identify Victor Clyde, if and when the police caught up with him.

There was news from a motel, complete with descriptions of Victor and Jessie. Their sojourn at the Commodore was high-lighted, omitting only the small contribution of facts from the two bellboys. The transaction between Victor and Paul Marron, the used-car dealer, was reported in full.

Victor read with a widening grin. So what have they got, he gloated. From the moment he bought the Buick in Yonkers in the name of William. V. Chase, the police were at a dead end. He had slipped out from under. Victor Clyde was *spurlos versenkt* and William Chase, complete with light-brown ragged eyebrows was free as air.

But no paper mentioned that Washington had identified him as Francis Edwards; that three detectives had flown out to Alma, Ohio; that Samuel Edwards, a decent, God-fearing man, on hearing the facts, had declared uncompromisingly that if his son came to him, with or without the child he had kidnaped, he would himself deliver the murderer to the police; or that he had provided them with a cabinet photograph of Francis Edwards, taken just before his embarkation to the Pacific; or that Samson, artist and police consultant, was at work on a drawing of Francis Edwards which would shortly hit the papers, police stations and post offices of every city, town, village and hamlet in America.

A little before three it occurred to Victor that he might gather his news even sooner than from the evening papers. He left the cafeteria, dropped another dime in the parking-meter, entered the first bar he saw, ordered a beer and waited for the three-o'clock newscast on TV. He discovered that there was no newscast at three, but the program in progress was interrupted long enough to give a bulletin to the effect that a man and woman were being held in Scranton, Pennsylvania, in the belief that they might be the missing "Bensons." But not a word about Sandy.

At five Victor went to the subway station—the uptown side this time—bought all the evening papers and got into his car. A policeman was hovering near, so he drove off without a glance at his papers. Time enough when he got home, he thought, savoring his coming pleasure like a child saving his dessert until after he had drunk his milk.

He found Jessie preparing dinner and, with no more than a greeting, went to the living room to enjoy his feast. If he had been angry when he read the morning papers, he was frothing now. Eighteen hours since he had committed the most stupendous, daring, spectacular crime of the century and not a line in the papers about it. He twisted on the TV set savagely and struck the 6:45 news right on the nose. But the announcer uttered no word about the kidnaping. He began to sweat. Why were they keeping mum about it? Where were the lousy reporters at a time like this?

Suddenly he slapped his thigh and laughed out loud. Of course! That dumb cop Wiley didn't know that Victor Clyde and the kidnaper were one and the same. The whole cream of the joke lay in that fact. While Wiley was straining his guts, nosing after Lee Mack's killer, here he was, large as life, snatching Wiley's own kid right out of his bed. And Wiley didn't even have sense enough to add up two and two. Somebody had to put him wise and who but Victor Clyde himself?

He would drive down to Manhattan after dinner and phone him from a pay station. Let them try to trace the call. He'd be back in his car before they even had the zone. On second thoughts, he discarded phoning, not because it was dangerous but because he knew that in every big case a number of cranks flooded Headquarters with phone calls, saying they knew the criminal, sometimes even confessing to the crime itself. No. He had to think of something better—something unmistakable. . . .

His idea came to him at the dinner table when Jessie was prattling about the kid preferring the dictionary to a story-book. He waited until she had brought up Sandy's tray, had washed the dishes and straightened the kitchen for the night. She came into the living room where he was turning from channel to channel, hunting for news dealing with the boy. After all, even if they didn't connect up Mack's killer with the kidnaping, a snatch was a snatch and newsworthy in its own right. Or was it because it was a cop's kid? Did they keep it dark because their faces were too red to admit that the unknown enemy was too much for them?

As the newscaster repeated the earlier item about the couple in Scranton, Jessie gave a small shocked exclamation and rose.

"What's the matter?" he asked.

"Nothing—I—I just don't like—I—think I'll wash my hair—" she stammered and fled. She had shown the same distaste for listening last night, he remembered, when Mack's memorial had been on. It had annoyed him then, but tonight it suited his plans very well. When he heard the water running upstairs, he set to work.

A few minutes later, the trapdoor opened. Sandy looked up and saw a pair of large black shoes on the top step. In panic, he retreated across the room and stood, quaking. All his fears of the "man," deliberately shunted during the day, rushed forward to overwhelm him. But some untapped well of courage flowed up to help him. By the time Victor had descended into the room, Sandy's little face was a smooth mask. As he looked at Victor, frank curiosity dawned in his eyes. Victor was wearing garden gloves and held a writing-pad, an envelope and a ball-point pen. He said, "I hear you read the dictionary for fun."

"Yes, sir," said Sandy in a small voice.

"Then I bet you can write a good letter."

"I don't know about that, sir."

"Your folks know your handwriting?"

"I don't know." (One of Lieutenant Wiley's precepts was: never give the enemy information.)

"Well, I'm letting you write 'em a letter."

A bird of hope began to beat its wings in Sandy's ears.

Or was it just his own heart-beats?

"Yes, sir," he said as stolidly as he could.

"There are certain things I want you to tell them."

"Yes, sir."

"First, you tell them your—ah—host is Victor Clyde. Got that?"

"Yes, sir."

"That mean anything to you?"

"No, sir."

Victor couldn't help strutting even before a child.

"Your father's combing the country for Victor Clyde, the man who killed Lee Mack."

"Yes, sir."

"You don't seem surprised."

"Well," said Sandy incautiously, "I didn't know your name but—"

"But you knew I killed Mack, did you?" His tone was silky. Sandy dropped his eyes. The well of courage was drying up. "That's pretty dangerous information for a boy to be carrying around. We mustn't let you carry it too far, must we?" His voice hardened. "Well, that's neither here nor there. You write this letter and say Victor Clyde's got you. You say also that if the police don't drop the case, you'll never get out of here alive."

Sandy swallowed a knot of terror in his throat. His voice was a squeak, "They never drop a murder case."

"That's rough on you," said Victor dryly.

"Look—mister—" He couldn't control the tears.

"Shut up! Your father's too free with his adjectives. Let's see how he likes it on the receiving end. Now then. You tell him Victor Clyde's got you. If you value your life, you don't say anything that could give him a lead to me—"

"I don't know anything," Sandy lied valiantly.

"No, I guess you don't at that. Another thing: I want him to be sure the letter's from you whether he knows your writing or not. See that you mention something—a toy—   or a pet—or some people— that only you and they can recognize. Understand?"

"Yes, sir."

Victor laid down the pad, envelope and pen.

"Get to work. Address the envelope, too, but don't seal it. I'll be down in half an hour to check on the letter before I mail it. Any tricks and you're a dead duck."

He went up the steps and the trapdoor closed with a soft thud.

The bird of hope started up again. This was the Game with a vengeance. The sub-cellar was an escape-proof prison which was physically impossible for a small boy to get out of. But here Sandy had a heaven-sent chance to send a Clue to his father, if only he was smart enough to devise one which would be clear enough to help his father but hidden enough to pass Victor's suspicious eye. Sandy had one definite fact to transmit. If he put it across, Lieutenant Wiley of Homicide would do the rest. He began to write.

CHAPTER TWENTY-ONE

Meg and Lance sat at the table, making heavy weather of eating breakfast. Meg had physically recovered from her experience of two nights ago. But a deeper sickness afflicted both her and Lance. It had been impossible to keep the news of Sandy from her and their only comfort was that they shared their trouble. But it was cold comfort. Things were at a bleak standstill. The Scranton tip had fizzled out; the couple were legitimately entitled to the name Benson and they had produced substantiated alibis, far from New York City, for the critical times of Mack's murder and the kidnaping of Sandy. The detectives watching the Edwards' farm had nothing to report. There was no sign of Francis Edwards there.

Thirty-two of the forty-eight hours' secrecy Lance had asked for had passed. He had only sixteen more in which to hope for a break of some kind. After that, Captain Manders would follow his own policy of publicity and give the news to the reporters. There had been the usual nuisance phone calls and letters to Headquarters about the Mack case but none of them had hinted at the kidnaping and were, therefore, not the lead Lance was looking for so hungrily. Hope was dying, a little at a time, as the hours passed and Francis Edwards made no move.

As he pushed his scrambled eggs around his plate, Lance said dismally, "I guessed wrong. I thought I had Edwards' mental processes down so pat. But it looks like self-preservation's stronger even than vanity. He won't dare to write or phone."

"I'm not so sure, Lance." Meg's face was white; she was nearly fainting with dread, but her voice was steady. It was important to keep Lance's morale up. Time enough after he left for the office to give way to her own feelings. "Stealing Sandy was an insane thing to do. And a madman isn't as concerned about his safety as much as about his self-importance. After all, it's only been one clear day since—since— Give him time—"

"Time is what we haven't got, darling!" He struck his hands together in a desperate gesture. "These hours of waiting—every minute—every second—a horrible danger—Manders is right—the risk's too great—I'll go down and talk to the reporters now—I won't wait—"

This was not the Lance she knew. This frantic man who had had no more than six hours' sleep in the last sixty hours since Lee Mack was killed needed something that Meg and Meg alone could give. She said steadily, "Lance, you're too tired to think straight. Remember how many times you've been right when you put yourself into a criminal's skin. Give your theory a chance—"

"If he was going to phone, he'd have done it by now."

"That's true. But if he writes— Don't you see? If he wrote yesterday, we couldn't possibly get it until today—"

"All right. I'll wait till the mail comes. If there's nothing, I'll go downtown. If there's nothing there either, I'll give it to the papers." He started to his feet and prowled the dining room. "If there was something to do. But we're at a dead stop. We don't know where to look. We don't know where to start. He's vanished into thin air. He's not going to Ohio. He's no gangster with underworld hide-outs. We'd have him on record if he was. He can be anywhere—anywhere—"

The front door chimes sounded. They both raced into the front hall. Three white envelopes dropped through the slot. The postman tramped away down the walk outside.

They both recognized Sandy's writing at the same instant as it lay face up on the floor. The sight had diverse effects. Lance straightened, galvanized into new vigor and purpose; Meg sagged and would have fallen if he had not caught her. He carried her to the living-room couch, then returned to the hall. With his handkerchief, he picked up the letter by one corner, carried it in to the coffee table in front of Meg, slit it with his knife without touching it and maneuvered until it spread open before them:

> *Dear Mommy and Daddy:*
> *The man says to tell you his name is Victor Clyde. He says who is stupid now. He says to tell you if you don't drop the case, I won't get out of here alive. I told him murder cases are never dropped just marked unsolved still open but that doesn't matter to him. Oh daddy don't they ever drop one if it would save my life? Being kidnaped isn't as bad as I expected. Nobody is mean to me and the food is very good but I am lonesome for you both. Oh, mommy, I wish we could all be together again and go for croffee and rolls at Elizabeth's house and I miss my space-suit awful much. Oh, daddy, please do what the man says.*
>
> *Sandy*

The tears were raining down Meg's cheeks and she sobbed uncontrollably. Lance held her close, cursing Victor Clyde. But he spoke soothingly, "Don't, darling. Pull yourself together. We were right! We forced him into sending a letter—it's something to start from—I have to get downtown with it—"

"Lance!" Her voice rose to near-hysteria. "They're drugging him! He's delirious—"

"No, darling—"

"Talking about Elizabeth—we don't know any

Elizabeth—and coffee—he never touched a drop in his life—"

"The rest of the letter's sane enough."

"I tell you he's out of his head—misspelling an easy word like coffee—"

Lance looked at her, at the letter and then gave an ungodly shout. It did what all his soothing had failed to do: Meg sat up, the tears stopped, her body ceased its trembling.

"Lance! What is it?" She eyed his electric energy with hope. She knew him when he had a lead.

"That blessed kid!" he said with actual laughter in his voice. "He's played the Game! He's handed me the Clue!"

"Lance—please—what do you—?"

"Darling—remember a day—oh, months ago— yes—we were going up to Lydia Carr's wedding—we got off the Parkway and took back roads—"

"Lance—get to the point!" She shook his arm.

"We passed a village—name of Crawfey and I did a little clowning—threw a handkerchief over my arm and pretended I was a waiter. I said 'Tea, cocoa, milk or Crawfey'—"

Meg sprang to her feet, her eyes wide.

"Yes! Yes! Yes! And the houses in the village—I told Sandy they were Elizabethan—"

"That caps it. Darling, I must go. I'll keep in touch."

Forty minutes later, Lance was finishing his story to Captain Manders and Gregory Peters of the FBI. Manders was skeptical.

"Now, don't go off half-cocked, Lance. Here's a kid, writing under pressure, scared stiff. So he puts an 'r' in the word coffee and you jump—"

"But he never tasted coffee—then the Elizabethan thing—and he and I make a thing about the Detective Game—there's always a Clue—"

Agent Peters cut in, quiet but incisive, "Captain,

Lieutenant Wiley was psychologically right about Edwards. The absence of publicity forced him into sending this letter. Let's go on the premise that he's right again."

"Well, of course, it's got to be investigated. We can't leave a pebble unturned, stymied as we are. Go to it, but don't expect too much." Then he held up a detaining hand. "Wait a minute—Lance, you're out of this deal—"

"Out?" echoed Lance unbelievingly.

"Out. This Edwards saw you on television. The boy's letter shows that. The moment he sees you—"

"Captain," said Lance stubbornly, "this is my case. I ask you to reconsider."

Manders was intensely sorry for Lance. It made him much gentler than usual, in view of Lance's insubordination.

"This is a ticklish operation, Lance. If the man's alerted, no telling what he might do to the boy."

"I'll take along my kit. You know what I can do with make-up. If we get as far as locating him, I guarantee he'll never recognize me."

"Why take the risk?"

"This is one job I've got to do myself, Captain." There was something in his tone that Manders could not combat. For the second time in the Victor Clyde case, the Captain gave in.

They used an unmarked black sedan for the ride to Crawfey, a plain-clothes man as driver, with Peters, Lance and Sergeant Knight in the back seat. They made good time on the Parkway. Then, at Lance's direction, they turned off onto a secondary narrower road through sparse communities and wooded sections. There was little traffic and they were still going along at a good clip when Hanson, the chauffeur, braked the car sharply. In the road stood a soldier holding up a sign which said: *Slow.*

Lance looked ahead and saw the reason. As far as

the eye could see on the winding road, army trucks were lined up on one side of the road. The huge parked trucks narrowed the road appreciably and Hanson slowed to a crawl as he drove by. It seemed to be a complete battalion, with guns, ammunition, hospital, field kitchen, gasoline trucks and even a police unit with a handful of prisoners. Under the trees at the sides of the road, hundreds of soldiers were deployed, smoking, relaxing and crossing from one side of the road to the other.

"Looks like we busted into a practice maneuver," Knight said.

"Either that or a battalion moving from one post to another," said Peters. "Seem to be halting for a meal."

"Probably an outfit from Fort Slocum," Hanson contributed. "It's not too far from here."

Only Lance said nothing. He was chafing at the trifling delay, counting the minutes, even the seconds that the slowdown was costing them. He thought the stationary column would go on forever. But after a couple of miles, it did finally end and Hanson sent the car ahead again at normal speed. They had lost about ten minutes but to Lance it seemed a lifetime. With a breath of relief, he went back to the job of directing. By and by, as the walls and gates of private estates flew by, his anxious face cleared.

"I remember all this. We're not far now. We'll come to a sign marked 'Crawfey. Settled seventeen something.'"

They did. They passed a golf course; then an unkempt property surrounded by a thick growth of trees with a small solid house set down in the middle of it; then a handsome high school; then a narrow main street, lined with quaint Tudor houses; and finally another small stone box of a building marked *Police Station*, a structure comparatively new to the district. A roomy stone garage stood behind it and the police driver, at Lance's direction, drove the car into it.

"We don't want anybody to see a New York City license if we can help it," he said.

It was nearly one o'clock when they entered the station house. The street was practically deserted. Crawfey was eating its midday dinner.

A good-looking blond boy of about twenty-three with alert eyes sat behind the desk in the office. He rose as the four men came in, masking his curiosity with an aplomb beyond his years. He addressed Peters, as the oldest of the group. "Yes, sir?"

"We would like to see the Chief of Police."

"Yes, sir. He's upstairs at his dinner. If you'll sit down, I'll fetch him."

While he was gone, Lance studied the layout. The office was comfortable and substantial. Across the hall, two cells, with barred doors (both now open) proclaimed that the building was jail as well as headquarters. A flight of stairs in the central hall evidently led up to the Chief's living quarters.

In a few minutes the boy returned with a man who might have stepped onto any stage as Falstaff without benefit of make-up. His cheeks were round and pink, his blue eyes were circled with laughter lines and his paunch was memorable. He gave his visitors a sharp glance and said, "Good day. I'm Harry Bell, Police Chief here. You wanted to see me?"

Peters identified them all, there was some handshaking and Bell said, "This is Derek Farthing, my deputy. You want he should go?"

"No, I don't think so. We've come on a very serious matter. Another head won't hurt," said Peters.

Lance told the story, keeping it strictly factual. When he came to the part about Sandy's "Clue," it shrank to the point of fantasy before this unimaginative stranger. Not that he was stupid but psychology was not in his stars. Lance finished, glossing over the Clue: "We have reason to believe that the, boy is being held captive here in Crawfey."

Harry Bell laughed, a rich, pleasant, infectious sound.

"Gentlemen, that is a sheer impossibility. I wish I could help you but it just isn't so. There's not a human being in Crawfey who would or could do such a thing."

"Why not?"

"You pass through the village? Then you saw how close the houses are built. You sneeze in one, and your neighbor says, 'God bless you.' You couldn't keep an active boy of eight an hour without the whole village knowing it."

"How about the surrounding estates?"

"Well, I'll tell you about that. There's a whole settlement of outlanders in the district. They're a godless crew, lunatics, some of 'em, mostly from New York City."

"Well, possibly one of them—" suggested Peters, deadpan.

"No," said Bell. "We don't pretend to like 'em here, but it couldn't be them neither."

"How can you be so sure?"

"I'll tell you about that, too," said Bell expansively. "Crawfey's got no industries and—" he added proudly, "consequently no slums. We don't get rich, I admit, but then we don't get adulterated, you might say."

"You've got a mighty handsome high school," said Peters.

"Oh, we taxed the foreigners for that. The truth is, gentlemen, they're our main means of support. They keep us going, buying Crawfey liquor and Crawfey hardware and groceries."

Lance had to keep a tight hold on himself as the garrulous Chief chattered on. "That's about all they're good for—"

"But they could still harbor a child," Lance broke in restively.

"They buy one more thing," said Bell, finally making his point. "They buy service. Our Crawfey boys are constantly in and out of every house around for miles—mending their power saws and power mowers and do-it-yourself gadgets that Hewitt's sticks 'em with. Or helping with their new-fangled strawberry and asparagus farms and such. And our girls have the run of every house, baby-sitting, helping with housework and waiting on table when they entertain each other at dinners. If a strange boy was being harbored in any house, our young folks would smell it out and I'd know it within an hour."

"The colony aside, has any stranger settled here recently?" Lance asked.

"Strangers don't seem to like Crawfey air," said Bell dryly. "They never last long." He moved in his chair as if to end the meeting. "Sorry to disappoint you, gentlemen, but—"

The boy, Derek Farthing, spoke for the first time: "Jess Hewitt's husband's a stranger."

"Who's Jess Hewitt?" Lance asked quickly; but Bell intervened: "Derek, you got a screw loose? Linking up Jessie Hewitt with a kidnaping!"

"Who is Jessie Hewitt?" Lance repeated.

Again it was Bell who answered: "You can forget Jessie Hewitt, sir. Why, there were grown Hewitts here in Crawfey before George Washington was born."

"Then she's got nothing to hide. Where does she live?"

"Hewitt's Farm down next to the high school," said Derek.

Lance remembered the unkempt grounds, the isolated little house and thought it could well hide secrets.

"Tell us about her," he said to the boy.

"Well, she was in my class at high. She was a nice kid but she had it rough. Her father used to beat her up for every little thing. She thought nobody knew about it but we did, all right, coming to school with her hair pulled down over her forehead and long sleeves to hide the marks."

"Did you know her well?"

"Nobody did because she didn't dast have friends at her house. And she was proud, too. Once I gave her a bag of candy after school. She threw it right back at me and she said: 'Don't you dare be sorry for me!' Then she took off so I shouldn't see she was starting to cry."

"You mentioned a husband—"

"Well, after she lit out for Hollywood—"

"Hollywood!" Lance exclaimed, galvanized, remembering Grotz. "When was this?"

"A year or so ago. She did real well, too—least, what she wrote back to Maud Chiltern and Orville Bayne. Said they were training her to be a big movie star."

"Go on."

"Then Mr. Fraser wrote her about her father's sickness and said she better come back. She came. And brought her husband with her."

"How long ago?"

"Let's see—Mr. Hewitt died the twentieth of March. Jess got here just in time for the funeral— maybe a few days before."

"Would you say about March fifteenth?" Lance asked breathlessly. Mr. and Mrs. Victor Clyde had checked out of the Commodore March fifteenth.

"About that."

"What's his name—the husband?"

"Chase."

Harry Bell cut in with authority: "All this is neither here nor there. Jessie's husband is a prosperous, respectable business man—"

"Was he away on Decoration Day?"

"Dec— Suppose he was? That's no cause to— Let me tell you this: he could be the blackest character under the sun—which he isn't—but if you think Jessie Hewitt'd stand for a cold-blooded dastardly kidnaping—"

"Will you describe him, please." Lance took another tack.

"He's a big fellow," said Bell with a resigned shrug. "Well-built. Honest open face, not what you call handsome but friendly and pleasant. And he is pleasant. I play poker with him and you can always tell a man's nature in a—"

"What sort of eyebrows has he got?"

"Eyebrows!" Bell looked startled. He went on slowly, "Well—now you mention it, they're real noticeable. Curved and kind of sweeping—"

"Not anymore!" Derek said in sudden excitement. They all turned to him and he went on, his eyes snapping, "I saw him in Hewitt's day before yesterday. I looked at him twice—he looked different—washed-out like—I couldn't lay a name to it—now I know—his eyebrows were paler and sort of moth-eaten—"

They finally convinced Harry Bell and once convinced, he was furious at Victor Chase and entirely co-operative.

"We've got to consider our approach," said Peters. "If he's alerted in any way, it's dangerous to the boy."

A silence fell while they all considered. At last, Lance, his eyes blank and fixed on the opposite wall, began to speak, aloud but half to himself, "Sandy was alive and well last night when he wrote the letter. But how much longer till Edwards realizes he's a deadly danger to him? Every hour is a risk. We can't wait even till dark to rush the place. But that driveway down to his house. The moment we turn in, he may get panicky and do away with Sandy. We've got to have a plan—" His eyes sharpened suddenly. He turned to Bell: "Where's the nearest Legion Post around here, do you know?"

Bell stared, then grinned.

"I ought to. I'm practically a charter member. Never missed a get-together since World War I."

"How close is it?"

"Kershaw. Nine miles from here."

Lance's eyes were snapping with excitement. "Charter member? Then you could ask a favor of them, I suppose?"

"Sure could."

"Fine. Now, one thing more, Mr. Bell. Would Chase take it amiss if he saw your car turn into his driveway?"

"Not a bit. I'm a bachelor and our poker game always meets at my place upstairs."

"Wouldn't he think it more natural for you to phone?"

"Nope. Sarah Griff, our telephone operator's the daughter of the local parson. She's a good listener-in. So if we don't want gambling to be the subject of the Reverend Griff's Sunday sermon, we don't use the phone for our—uh—arrangements."

"Good." Lance turned, addressing them all, "Now here's what I have in mind. . . ."

CHAPTER TWENTY-TWO

Over another breakfast table that morning, anxiety had reigned too. Victor and Jessie ate silently. Reaction had set in, in Victor's mind. Now that he had had his fun at Lance Wiley's expense, his unruly second-self had subsided, leaving his problems for Victor to solve. They were nearly unsolvable, he admitted reluctantly to himself, although he would never in the world admit it to Jessie.

The boy was a white elephant. Worse. He was a millstone around Victor's neck. He would have been delighted to keep his promise to Jessie and drop the child out of the car a hundred miles away, for somebody to pick up and restore to his parents. But it was too risky. Although he was convinced that Sandy had no idea of his whereabouts, the boy knew him by sight and could point him out. It wasn't too likely that Victor's path and that of a kid of eight living in Riverdale would ever cross. But what kind of a life would that be, knowing that at any time in the whole of his future, his freedom and his life could be jeopardized by a glance from a small boy?

Victor could be driving along a highway, he could be buying a pair of socks, he could be having a haircut, and the long arm of coincidence could clutch at him and squeeze him to death. Silently, he cursed Lance Wiley for his television insults, cursed the boy for the fact that he had eyes and ears. Stealthily, a sweet suggestion eased his worry if the boy didn't have eyes and ears, or a tongue to accuse with, Victor Clyde wouldn't have to skulk in a God-forsaken hole like Crawfey for the rest of his life.

Jessie's voice broke in on his musing, "Will it be tonight, Vic?"

He started guiltily. "What?"

"We can't keep him forever."

"Forever!" he gibed. "He hasn't been here two days."

"Well, it's long enough to make me a nervous wreck."

"What's to be nervous about?" He laughed with hollow heartiness. "We could have a house full of callers and the kid could yell his lungs out down there and nobody'd hear. Your grandpa did a damn good job of soundproofing, when you consider he built the place close to forty years ago."

It wasn't the happiest subject to bring up. At mention of her grandfather, a wave of incredulity and unreality swept over her: how on earth could Emery Hewitt's granddaughter have been maneuvered into such a spot? But it passed and it was Victor Chase's devoted wife who spoke: "Darling, every hour he's here is a danger to you. Please do it tonight." She reached across the table and clutched his hand. "Vic, we've got troubles enough without this—I'm so afraid—"

"Oh, cut the nagging, Jessie."

"Once Sandy's gone, I'll be a different person. I can't bear cooping him up down there—"

He sat up indignantly. "Well, for God's sake! So you're sorry for him!"

Her lips were quivering but she answered steadily enough: "Yes, I'm sorry for him, Vic. A thing like this could haunt a kid—darken his whole childhood—I know what it's like to shiver with fear—and be too little to fight back."

The shrewd side of Victor recognized this danger in his own house. He'd have to get rid of Sandy before the unreliable Jessie made a real issue of it and put Victor on a hell of a spot. Not that she would ever deliberately betray him, but in his estimation she was still the "crazy mixed-up kid" who had to be controlled and managed and guided carefully wherever he decided to lead. He managed her now with practiced ease. He gave her one of his sweet enveloping smiles and poured it on: "Poor little Jessie. You sure had it rough. But that's all over the dam. Anybody tries to hurt the nail on your little finger, they've got me to reckon with. I personally am guaranteeing you'll never have another unhappy day in your life."

"I know. I know." Her breath caught with her grateful appreciation. But she was still Jessie Hewitt. "And Sandy—?"

"I'll get him out of here tonight."

"You promise?"

"I promise. That okay, baby?"

"Oh, darling, yes! I knew you would."

He drove down to New York after breakfast as much to get away from Jessie as to buy the morning papers.

On the way home, he, too, was slowed down by the National Guard battalion but he felt none of the intolerable tension that Lance had felt. He eyed the outfit with interest, even a faint nostalgia for his own army days, and drove by leisurely, in no rush to get home.

By three o'clock he was back. Jessie, playing checkers with Sandy, heard his car coming down the driveway to the house. Her instinct told her that fraternizing with the boy was not wise at this time when Victor was so close to granting her her wishes. Hastily she said to Sandy, "I've got to stop now." She ran up the steps, dropped the trapdoor, replaced the carton over it and hurried to the kitchen so that she would be innocently occupied when Victor came in.

But Victor didn't come in. Instead, he ran the car into the garage, went to the tool shed and emerged in coveralls and carrying something she could not see. Mystified, she watched him walk back toward the densest growth of trees surrounding the house. Half an hour later, he reappeared. He was carrying a shovel. He started for the tool shed but Jessie threw open the kitchen door and called, "Vic! What on earth are you—?"

He rushed up the kitchen steps, his face dark with anger.

"Stop your yelling! You want to rout out the neighborhood?"

He slammed the muddy shovel in a corner and pushed past her, muttering: "Got to clean up." He was wet with perspiration and earth clung to his shoes.

A lightning flash of blinding horror struck her. "Victor, no!" she screamed. "You can't! You can't do this—"

He brushed her off and was halfway up the front stairs with Jessie babbling and clinging to him, when he froze suddenly at an outside sound.

"Car coming down the drive," he croaked. "See who it is."

In spite of her horror she automatically fell into her usual obedience. She peered through the lace-covered panel of the front door.

"It's only Harry Bell," she panted. "Vic, listen—"

"All right. All right. Later. Calm down and let him in. I'll be right down." He raced up the stairs.

By some miracle, she was composed again by the time Harry Bell rang and she let him in, but her face was a waxy yellow.

"Oh, hello, Harry. Come in." She hardly cast a glance at the two men who stood behind him; men in the uniform of the United States Army but with the broad arm band marking them as Military Police. The tall spare one with inscrutable eyes seemed to be the leader. The other one, with plumped-out cheeks like a squirrel and a dense oily mop of black hair which began low on his forehead and straggled out from under his cap, seemed content to remain in the background. Meg herself would not have recognized him.

"How you been, Jessie?" Bell asked affably.

"All right, thanks."

"Vic around?"

There was a sharp hiss as the black-haired man drew in his breath. Vic. That clinched it. Luckily, Jessie's voice smothered the sound.

"Yes. He's upstairs. He'll be right down."

"Gettin' ready with that famous coconut cake of yours for the Fair?"

"That's right," she said with mechanical brightness. "It starts on the fifth of June."

Victor appeared on the stairs, minus the coveralls and sufficiently neat and at ease. Harry gave him a friendly salute: "Hi, Vic. No, this ain't an invite to a game." He indicated the man beside him. "This is Sergeant Peters of the 66th Battalion."

"That right?" said Vic cordially. "What can I do for him?" He remembered the line of army trucks he had passed coming home, and never doubted the truth of Bell's statement.

"Well, his outfit was parked down the road for a lunch break a while ago and it seems they lost a man. Strolled into the bushes and right on over the hill."

Victor came down the stairs.

"So?"

"Well, naturally, the M.P.'s got on the job, asking around. And Sergeant Peters here hit the jackpot. The pro next door saw a soldier cross the golf course, tramping all over the green with his G.I. boots and ran after him to shoo him off. So the soldier takes off through the trees, smack in the direction of this house. You see or hear anything of him?"

"Not a sign."

"You, Jessie?"

"No." There was a sudden queer light in her eyes. "But he might have got in without my hearing him. Our doors are never locked."

"That's what I figured."

"He'd be an awful sucker to come into a house with all the woods around here to hole up in," said Vic.

"Sergeant" Peters spoke for the first time: "He'd be after civvies. If he don't get out of uniform fast, he's dead."

Vic nodded. "I get it. You want to search the house."

"Yes, sir."

"Go to it. I'll give you a hand."

"That's very co-operative of you, sir."

Vic grinned. "Hell, chances are the guy's heeled. You're doing me the favor. I know nicer things than tangling with an AWOL kid with an Army Issue gun." Lance, unobtrusive in the background, was filled with misgiving. The man was entirely too much at ease. If a search could turn up any sign of Sandy, there should have been some disquiet in Victor, no matter how well masked. It argued that Sandy was not on the premises and that was a thought with ghastly conclusions in its wake. But offsetting Victor's calm, it seemed to Lance that the girl had been stiff with fear when she let them in, before ever there had been mention of the AWOL soldier. He was sure he had the right man. So much pointed to it. Victor Clyde, Victor Chase; Derek's story of the camouflaged eyebrows; the fact that Jessie had met him in California; Sandy's "croffee" clue. He felt he had Lee Mack's murderer but that was secondary. At the moment it was Sandy who counted. He came back to the present as Victor was saying, "Where you want to start?"

"There's enough of us to cover the house all at once," said Bell. "Vic, you and me take the attic, Sergeant Peters can go over the bedroom floor and the other one can mosey around the cellar. I'll just make sure of this floor before we start." He made a tour of the dining room and kitchen and returned to them in the living room. "Nobody down here. No place to hide, 'less he could squinch himself in the oven. Let's go."

Victor led Peters and Bell up the front stairs. Lance and Jessie stood silent until he said, "If you'll show me the way to the cellar, ma'am—"

She started as if she had hardly been aware of her surroundings. Her distraction gave him a tiny hope that Sandy was here. Perhaps Victor was a consummate actor and hid all traces of guilt. Or did he count on eluding them all and making a dash for it if they found Sandy? That didn't trouble Lance with Sergeant Knight outside the front door, Derek Farthing and the police chauffeur at the back and a State Police roadblock covering every route out of the village.

Jessie said quietly, "Oh, certainly. The cellar door is in the kitchen."

She led the way to the clean, bright, attractive kitchen. The room simply did not go with the concept of kidnaping. Jessie's eyes went to the corner of the room and her body went tense. Lance followed her look and was newly puzzled. All he saw was a muddy shovel on her immaculate linoleum. Another "Craig's Wife," he wondered, asking himself if he had been all wrong about her. Had it been irritation and not fright in the girl's face?

She opened the cellar door and turned on a switch.

"Down those steps," she said in a flat tone.

Lance found himself in an orderly cellar with whitewashed walls and everything in its place except for an open good-sized carton in one corner with excelsior spilling out of it. It had once contained a television set, he saw, but now held only a heavy rusted iron anvil. He searched every cranny of the cellar but found nothing. He even performed the gruesome chore of digging down through the excelsior of the carton to satisfy himself that there was no dreadful inanimate secret there.

But he did not move it from its corner.

When he came up into the kitchen again, Peters was there with Jessie.

"Nothing in the cellar," he told Peters. A moment later, Victor and Bell clattered down the wide oak stairs and came in.

"All clear in the attic," Bell announced. "Jessie, don't look so scared. I personally raised the lid of every last trunk up there."

Victor slipped an arm around Jessie and led her to a chair.

"My wife's not feeling too well. And this business certainly hasn't done her any good. Sit down, honey. There's nothing to worry about."

She sank into the chair without speaking and Victor stood behind her, one hand on her shoulder. He said, "Harry, you might give the tool shed and the garage the once-over before you go, just to satisfy Jessie. Myself, I think that pro next door was only looking for some limelight."

"We'll do that," Bell said and moved across the kitchen toward the front hall. Lance could read the "I-told-you-so" look in Bell's eyes. The police Chief had switched back to his first belief that Vic Chase and especially Jessie Hewitt could not be involved in a kidnaping.

Peters's face was more inscrutable but he shrugged almost imperceptibly. The shrug said: "Hard luck, old man, but it looks like you guessed wrong." He, too, moved toward the door to the front hall after Bell.

Heartsick, dizzy with blinding frustration, Lance stood rooted, unable to give up. Victor Chase, if he was Victor Clyde, would be boxed in and easy to capture even if they left. But every nerve in Lance's body screamed against leaving him alone in the house with . . . what? Harry Bell called to him, "Come on, young man. He may have holed up in the high school next door. Let's go."

Then Jessie was on her feet, crying breathlessly, "Oh, wait—there's one place—the sub-cellar under the trap door—"

They were the last words she ever spoke. Behind her, Victor's gun roared, activated by his raging second-self.

Jessie sank slowly, almost as if she were making a curtsey, and then lay still in a little heap. Before she was halfway down, Lance shot the gun out of Victor's hand before it could be turned on the rest of them. With a scream, Victor threw himself on the floor, bellowing with pain, his legs flailing like a bad child in a tantrum. Harry Bell, horror-stricken, and now in no mood for benevolence, snapped handcuffs on his wrists, none too gently. Peters, cooler and more objective, bandaged Victor's ruined fingers lest he bleed to death before due process of law caught up with him.

Lance, with Jessie's words ringing in his ears, tore down the cellar steps. In an instant, the purpose of the weighted carton became clear and he shoved it aside. It took him a little longer to locate the spring that worked the trapdoor but not too long. As it rose silently, he snatched off the wig and the plumpers that stretched his cheeks. If Sandy was all right, no use frightening him further . . .

He was down the second flight of steps and Sandy was swarming up him, twining around his neck, laughing and crying, "Daddy! I knew you'd come! You guessed the Clue!"

There are times when a man may cry, too. They clung together for long moments. Then Lance mopped both their faces and talked quietly to Sandy until the call, "All Clear," came from above. Lance knew this meant that they had removed both Jessie and Victor from the kitchen, so that the boy need undergo no further horrors on his way out to freedom.

"Come on, young Sandy. We'll let Mommy know you're safe."

The phone was in the kitchen as in many country homes. Lance rang Meg and gave her the news. It was hard to convince her that everything was all right. Lance said, "Here, I'll let you talk to him," and handed the phone to Sandy.

"Hello, Mommy—I'm not kidnaped any more—

sure, I'm fine—only my pajamas are awful dirty—and the only baths I had were in little hunks— Oh, and Mommy, I had a dictionary and I can spell 'asafetida'—you want me to spell it for you?"

He spelled it.

Later that night, with all the loose ends of the case trimly tied, Sandy was sleeping as tranquilly as if Victor Clyde had never existed. Meg was straightening up the bathroom after his tempestuous bath. She picked up the little red knitted slippers which Sandy had worn home from Crawfey and she thought of the unhappy muddled girl who had given her life so that Sandy could live. Tears splashed on the slippers—tears for Jessie Hewitt.

THE END

Edna Solomon Sherry was born in Cincinnati, Ohio, on November 28, 1885. She graduated from Hunter College in 1906 and taught English there before becoming a professional writer. She began writing short stories for the pulp magazines, collaborating with Milton Gropper on two early novels. Sherry's first crime novel—and best known work—is *Sudden Fear*, published in 1948. It was filmed in1952 with Joan Crawford, Jack Palance and Gloria Grahame, and is considered a film noir classic. Sherry married dentist Ernest Sherry in 1909, and remained so until his death. Sherry herself passed away on February 4, 1967, in New York City.

Black Gat Books

Black Gat Books is a new line of mass market paperbacks introduced in 2015 by Stark House Press. New titles appear every other month, featuring the best in crime fiction reprints. Each book is size to 4.25" x 7", just like they used to be, and priced at $9.99. Collect them all.

1 Haven for the Damned
   by Harry Whittington
   978-1-933586-75-5
2 Eddie's World
   by Charlie Stella
   978-1-933586-76-2
3 Stranger at Home
   by Leigh Brackett
   writing as
   George Sanders
   978-1-933586-78-6
4 The Persian Cat
   by John Flagg
   978-1933586-90-8
5 Only the Wicked
   by Gary Phillips
   978-1-933586-93-9
6 Felony Tank
   by Malcolm Braly
   978-1-933586-91-5
7 The Girl on the Bestseller
   List
   by Vin Packer
   978-1-933586-98-4
8 She Got What She Wanted
   by Orrie Hitt
   978-1-944520-04-5
9 The Woman on the Roof
   by Helen Nielsen
   978-1-944520-13-7
10 Angel's Flight
   by Lou Cameron
   978-1-944520-18-2

11 The Affair of Lady
   Westcott's Lost Ruby /
   The Case of the Unseen
   Assassin by Gary Lovisi
   978-1-944520-22-9
12 The Last Notch
   by Arnold Hano
   978-1-944520-31-1
13 Never Say No to a Killer
   by Clifton Adams
   978-1-944520-36-6
14 The Men from the Boys
   by Ed Lacy
   978-1-944520-46-5
15 Frenzy of Evil
   by Henry Kane
   978-1-944520-53-3
16 You'll Get Yours
   by William Ard
   978-1-944520-54-0
17 End of the Line
   by Dolores &
   Bert Hitchens
   978-1-9445205-7
18 Frantic
   by Noël Calef
   978-1-944520-66-3
19 The Hoods Take Over
   by Ovid Demaris
   978-1-944520-73-1
20 Madball
   by Fredric Brown
   978-1-944520-74-8

21 Stool Pigeon
   by Louis Malley
   978-1-944520-81-6
22 The Living End
   by Frank Kane
   978-1-944520-81-6
23 My Old Man's Badge
   by Ferguson Findley
   978-1-9445208-78-3
24 Tears Are For Angels
   by Paul Connelly
   978-1-944520-92-2
25 Two Names for Death
   by E. P. Fenwick
   978-195147301-3
26 Dead Wrong
   by Lorenz Heller
   978-1951473-03-7
27 Little Sister
   by Robert Martin
   978-1951473-07-5
28 Satan Takes the Helm
   By Calvin Clements
   978-1-951473-14-3
29 Cut Me In
   by Jack Karney
   978-1-951473-18-1
30 Hoodlums
   by George Benet
   978-1-951473-23-5
31 So Young, So Wicked
   by Jonathan Craig
   978-1-951473-30-3

Stark House Press

1315 H Street, Eureka, CA 95501 707-498-3135
griffinskye3@sbcglobal.net www.starkhousepress.com
Available from your local bookstore or direct from the publisher.

"Finally, here it is! A suspense novel as gripping as *The Desperate Hours*... a thriller which ranges from California to New York and fills all its pages with that 'I can't put it down' feeling."
—*Springfield News & Leader*

"Certain to keep the reader up beyond his bedtime."
—*San Francisco Call Bulletin*

"Superb!"
—*Columbus Dispatch*

"Miss Sherry displays a remarkable flair for plot; she can whip up a story as full of twists as a corkscrew..."
—*The Boston Globe*

"The novel is modeled on inverted detective novels since we know exactly how the crimes are committed and we follow the criminal's point of view for most of the narrative. However the book is not without a smattering of genuine detective work."
—J. F. Norris, *Pretty Sinister Books*

Edna Sherry Bibliography
(1885-1967)

Novels:

Is No One Innocent? (1930; with Milton
    Herbert Gropper, based on their play,
    Inspector Kennedy)
Grounds for Indecency (1931; with Milton
    Herbert Gropper)
Sudden Fear (1948)
No Questions Asked (1949)
Backfire (1956; reprinted in paperback as
    Murder at Nightfall)
Tears for Jessie Hewitt (1958; reprinted in
    paperback as *She Asked for Murder*)
The Defense Does Not Rest (1959)
The Survival of the Fittest (1960)
Call the Witness (1961)
Girl Missing (1962)
Strictly a Loser (1965)

Short Stories:

"The Crimson Girl" (with Charles K. Harris;
    Munsey's Magazine, March 1927)
"Strange Cargo" (with Charles K. Harris;
    Sweetheart Stories, Jan 24 1928)